Death by Crockpot

A Kissing Bridge Enchanted Book Cafe Mystery

By
Linda West

Linda West

Dedicated to my dear friend

Roseanne

What people are saying about:

Death
by
Crockpot

"Side-splittingly funny and great little thriller. West gives Evanovich a run for her money. Loved this book. Can't wait for the next. Thank you!"

Posie Arnold Entertainment Now

"A gripping fun suspense thriller and cozy mystery. Set in a small ski town and centered around a magical bakery. This is humorous American literature at its best."

Dan Collins Dartmouth

"5***** "Funny! I laughed out loud. This book is unique and page turning. Highly recommended!"

S. Sprawling FutureTrends

"A humorous lighthearted cozy mystery that is full of suspense and twists and turns that will leave you laughing and surprised. Kat O'Hara returns home penniless, heartbroken and without a job. When the magical Landers sisters hire her to run their new Enchanted Cafe little do they suspect that a gruesome murder is about to take place in their small town of Kissing Bridge Mountain. Things bubble over at the big chili cook-off when a crockpot goes missing and a body is found. Loved it!"

Joy Stella Buffalo, NY

"5****** Love these characters and so happy to see them return in another fun series! What a treat. Keep writing about Kissing Bridge please!"

Dawn Deviso Youngstown,

CHAPTER 1

Coming home to Kissing Bridge was mostly uneventful, except for the murder of poor Mrs. Olympus. A coyote got her. Dad was devastated.

Other than that sad affair, today was a beautiful typical winter day on the mountain. The sun was shining and a new snow had fallen during the night so it shone all pretty and pure. It sparkled with silver hints that belied the ice blue beneath.

I ambled down the quaint main street that led through the center of the small town of Kissing Bridge with a miserable look on my face. I was right back where I had started two months ago when I left. Heartbroken, penniless, and now *officially* - a cat woman.

Dad had named the old feral cat he'd fed daily in our garden, Mrs. Olympus. He couldn't bear to part with her kittens, after the wounds from the coyote attack proved fatal. By the time I got home from Paris, Dad was as attached to those five furry felines as any manly-man could be. When I found out he had named them all after the goddesses of Olympus, a fitting ode to their mother, I knew they were staying for good.

That was fine with me. Since my mother had died we were really missing some softness and femininity around the house. We needed some girl energy – *even cat ones.* I was a tomboy, and Dad was a good old-fashioned pub rat from Dublin. I also was not in the best place of my life – *to say the least.*

I reached a new low even for me, when I got a misdemeanor last week for doing donuts in an abandoned parking lot during a blizzard. In my defense, I had gotten stuck in a sudden storm when I went down to Six Pines to check out the venue space for the big chili cook-off. Carol, my boss, needed to know our booth position, and how many electrical sockets it had nearby.

The radio announced blizzard warnings, and a *driving ban* in effect. That meant, I wasn't allowed on the road to go backup the mountain road home to Kissing Bridge. What was a not-too-smart, rebellious cat woman supposed to do?

I was stuck in my 1985 Ford pick up truck, marooned in

an abandoned parking lot, staring at the base of Eagle's Peak mountain waiting for the snow to let up so I could go home. I wasn't planning on going anywhere. Honest.

I pulled off my ski cap, and rustled my long dark hair. I looked at myself in the mirror and sighed. My hair was stuck up oddly at the bottom, and was smooshed at the top from wearing the knit cap too long. Well, lucky me I wasn't going on any dates with this hairdo. I pushed my bangs down over my prominent forehead. My violet eyes stared back at me in the rearview mirror. I wondered how long I was going to be stuck in this Six Pines parking lot waiting for the darn driving ban to lift?

In retrospect, I should have just ignored the warnings, and hightailed it up the mountain road home. Instead, *I obeyed the law*, and I turned on a good classic radio channel, and let myself be absorbed in a morose Carpenter song. Recalling the story of her death made me even sadder about the death of my relationship with Lance. I switched the channel to a rock station. Before I knew it, I was the only car left in the parking lot, and one of those beers in the backseat just got *unpopped.*

Okay to be absolutely clear. *No one* was left in the parking lot but me. Essentially I was stuck, and sad, and pathetic - so I took the opportunity. Anyone in Kissing Bridge would have done the same. These Six Pines Valley people are really uptight let me tell you.

I took a quick check around, to make sure I was alone, then revved up the engine of my truck, and smashed that gas peddle to the floor. After I picked up enough speed on the icy ground, I slammed on the breaks and spun that little Ford pickup in the tightest fastest donut 360 - *three times in a row!*

I skidded to a stop a few moments later.

It was epic! Truly I wish someone had a camera! Why is it someone always seems to have one when you don't want one in your face?

I pulled out again, and spun a few more donuts with a huge smile plastered on my face. Doing the donuts made me feel alive, and strong and rebellious. I mentioned the beer right?

I spanned the empty snow laden parking lot, and I was still the only idiot outside in this weather. I figured I might as well do a few more spins, what was the harm? Perfect donut conditions like this was the kind of opportunity that may never come my way again. It was amazing.

Except for Fuzzbottom.

Det. Fuzzbottom, pulled me over just as I finished a wicked spin culminating in a hundred foot skid. I was still hand pumping cheering for myself singing, *"We will, we will rock you,"* when he knocked on my window to get my attention.

I rolled it down, and smiled. "Did you see that donut man? That was awesome!"

Fuzzbottom didn't smile back.

The detective from Six Pines took one look at me, and didn't feel so thrilled about my donut turning abilities. Even after I batted my violet eyes and said,

"I do declare."

Nothing.

The eye batting was useless. That move always worked for Scarlett O'Hara, it has *yet* to work for me. According to the officer, officially *not driving and drinking* in a car is still illegal.

I swear I wasn't a bit tipsy. Okay - maybe I laughed when I read his name tag and that didn't help my case. But Det. Fuzzbottom looked like a younger uglier version of Nicolas Cage with a bad attitude. He had a flat nose and his eyes were a weird muddy brown, and his name was *Fuzzbottom.* Come on! I'd laugh if I hadn't had a beer. Not to mention the hair.

Fuzzbottom had more hair on his face and body than any human I had ever seen. He could easily have gone as the wolf man to a Halloween party without any makeup. I was enthralled with how thick the dark hair was that seemed to sprout from his chest and up to the top of his neck like a reverse beard. Oddly his chin and jaw were devoid of any hair, and only his five o'clock shadow foretold he had shaved.

He didn't like me staring at his hairiness I guess, because he gave me a ticket. It seemed that any amount of drinking and driving was against the law, even if it's merely spinning donuts in an empty parking lot - go figure.

On top of everything else, now my license was suspended for six months and I had to pay a fine. Now, I could add - *no transportation*, to my long list of problems.

Luckily for me, the wonderful Landers ladies had decided to expand their cookie empire and open up a new café right next to their famous Landers' Bakery. They needed a server to work part time. It was right down the street from where I lived, so I could just walk to work.

Plus I got free meals.

CHAPTER 2

I stirred the ground up clove into the depths of the crockpot, and wished that I would have known. Then maybe I could have just heaved the darn thing out the window, or buried it in the backyard. But it was too late for that now.

It was an old crockpot. It was red with bits of gold scrolls worn off on the side from lots of use and from being well loved. In the center of the pot the gold insignia of CL declared to one and all that this was *Carol Landers'* personal crockpot. I was honored she was letting me use it to test out my new recipe for the chili contest. I felt a bit like Carol's crockpot these days, I'd seen years of use and felt a bit worn.

I'm not really over the hill by traditional age standards; I've just been through a lot lately. Yes, I'm over thirty, but thirty is the new twenty, *at least that's what I've heard.*

I definitely act like I'm in my twenties if I don't exactly look like it. I'm naturally immature and rebellious. Despite all my hopes to emulate my elegant Parisian born mother, I'm still more like my marathon beer-drinking dad, thanks to that O'Hara blood.

I went over to the spice shelf to get the next ingredient for the chili recipe. Cinnamon? Who would of thought to add that to chili? Still I wasn't going to question the cooking skills of the Landers sisters. Town gossip swore they had a magical recipe book that was passed down from their wacky mother that had helped them reign as baking queens in Kissing Bridge for over seventy years. Mysteriously, the magic was said to have also come with a curse that had kept them all single - until recently.

A year ago they opened *Landers' Bakery* and it became the most popular place in town to eat and hang out. People traveled from all over Vermont to sample their famous blue ribbon winning baked goods.

The bakery was as adorable and quaint as you would imagine on Kissing Bridge Mountain. Its cheery red and white curtains, and windows full of cookies and cakes, were a kiss of sunshine on a sleepy main street dusted with snow. You just couldn't walk by the Landers' Bakery without being enveloped in smells that warmed your soul, drifting jauntily from the kitchen and the delicious baked goods.

Once inside the bakery, you were sure to run into a friend or neighbor. The tables were long and roughhewn so groups of people could sit down together and chat without worry. Most everyone in Kissing Bridge was acquainted in some fashion or another anyway so why not just push all the tables together?

Every day the Landers' Bakery was packed with the town folk of Kissing Bridge. Young and old alike could be found coming in and out of the bakery, tinkling the bell at the door. They clutched brown paper bags filled with sweets, hot drinks, or sandwiches to take backup to the mountain skiing.

Business was so good, the Landers decided to expand. They bought the little shop next door and planned to open a new full menu restaurant, aptly named The *Enchanted Cozy Café*.

The whole town was talking about the upcoming grand opening of the new Landers endeavor. Reservations were piling up, and the guest list was already full for months..

CHAPTER 3

We had not officially opened the Enchanted Cozy Café yet, but people kept stopping by and peering in the windows with curiosity. They tapped on the door and asked to know when the big grand opening was, and what might be on the new menu.

The Landers' Bakery was attached to the new restaurant by way of the kitchens. There was a red door that allowed the staff to go back and forth between the kitchens of the two shops easily. Right now I had to go back into the bakery kitchen to use the refrigerator until the café got the last of the big equipment delivered tomorrow. The big opening was almost upon us.

I pushed through the dividing door back into the café, with a bowl full of carrots from the bakery pantry. I spotted Mr. Maritime looking into the front window. He was peering in curiously as if he was looking for someone. The CLOSED sign was up, but he jiggled the door handle anyway.

Mr. Maritime was a dressed in a tan suit with a matching overcoat, and he looked very stylish but stressed. His usual broad smiling mouth was pulled tight and he kept looking down the street as if he were expecting someone. He waved half-heartedly to me when he saw me, then reached into his pocket quickly, and withdrew his cell phone. Whoever was on the phone must have really upset him because he started throwing his hands in the air and screaming.

I tried not to stare, but he was yelling so loudly I could hear him through the glass. "Listen to me! I mean it! Over my dead body!" His face filled with a deep maroon red as if he was on the verge of a heart attack. I wondered if I should see if he was okay?

Just then, a brown UPS truck pulled up outside and parked. I put the bowl of carrots on the counter and went to unlock the door. We'd been waiting for this delivery for two weeks. I couldn't wait to tell the Landers.

As I unlocked the door for the deliveryman, I noticed that Mr. Maritime was sweating now, despite the cold weather, and he kept wiping his face with a handkerchief. He finally turned away in a huff, and started across the street. I opened the door, just in time to hear him yell, "I'll kill you for this, I swear it!"

I gasped and pulled back from the front door in case he turned and caught me so close, and within earshot. But he didn't look back. He continued across the road and got into his black BMW and sped away *too fast* for the main street of Kissing Bridge. I poked my head through the cracked door and looked after him, baffled by his odd behavior.

I heard a loud. "Humph!" Come from a few feet away.

I looked over, and smiled at Maxine. She was lounging in the front door of her shop next door, as usual, and she shook her head at the speedy departure of Mr. Maritime.

Maxine White was the owner of *Scrapbook Heaven*, a scrapbooking shop that was just across the little alley next to the cafe, and one of my favorite people.

Max was a female version of Liberace. She always had on some fantastical outfit and a look of disdain. I didn't know what color her natural hair was because she always wore different colored wigs. Today she had on a bright green wig, with a matching long slinky sequined dress. She took a sip from her teacup, and gestured to a family just walking into the *Travel and Realty* store across the street.

"Kids around here. He shouldn't be driving like that."

I agreed. "Totally. I wonder what's up with him?"

I had no idea what had gotten into nice Mr. Maritime. I knew his family and his daughter Diana; we had gone to school together. I had been to their house many times for birthday swim parties. The Maritimes had all girls, triplets - Diana, Delia and Deidra.

The girls had summer birthdays, and the Maritimes had one of the only inground pools in the town of Kissing Bridge. Mr. Maritime had always been polite, easygoing, and mild mannered, if not busy and distracted. Maybe I just didn't know him as well as I thought. Still, Diana and I had been extra close, and she never mentioned her father having a bad temper.

I shook the thought out of my head as I spotted the deliveryman get out of the UPS truck. He was a stocky bald guy wearing a brown uniform, and his arms were laden down with a pile of boxes.

I swung the door open wide, and smiled from ear to ear. "Thanks," I said. "Just put them over there."

He went inside and piled the five matching boxes on the floor by the counter. I was so excited I clapped my hands together in glee.

"Got the packages finally I see." Maxine cooed lounging from her doorframe.

I nodded happily. "Thank goodness! I was so afraid they weren't going to get here in time. Ethel's special order held the delivery up for over a month. You know how she is about her colors."

Maxine's laughter tinkled out like waves of sunshine. "Oh yes I certainly do. Well how fabulous then that they came just in time for the big contest!"

I breathed a sigh of relief. "No kidding!"

I waved goodbye to Maxine and closed the door. I had to get things ready for the big cook-off!

CHAPTER 4

There were five boxes in all. Each had a crockpot in it, and each of those crockpots was a different color. There would be five of us representing the new Enchanted Cozy Café at the big Chili Cook-Off in Six Pines next week. We were each responsible for our own colored crockpot. *Keep it warm, keep it filled, and keep serving.*

Dodie Anderson, was the manager next door at the Landers' Bakery, her crockpot was white. Summer Landers, Ethel's daughter, was assigned the yellow one. Ethel Landers would be wielding her signature Tiffany blue crockpot, made especially for her (that's why it took so long for them to get delivered) and I was delegated the black one, by default, nothing to do with my person mind you. Carol Landers would be using her signature lucky red crockpot.

We had ordered Carol an additional *red crockpot* especially for the contest, so she didn't have to use her own personal crockpot. Except if we needed backups.

Officially we were going to have the grand opening event of the Enchanted Cozy Cafe the *week after* the big Six Pines Chili Cook-Off. Our plan was to win the cook-off on Saturday, and then pass out coupons for the grand opening the following week. We hoped to fill the place to the brim on opening night and introduce hundreds of new customers to our place!

Kissing bridge was a twenty-minute drive up the mountain, but after a taste of the goods at the cook-off - coupled with a 50% coupon, we felt certain we could stir the crowd to make the drive up to Kissing Bridge Mountain. Plus as winners we would be all over the TV, allowing us even more free press.

I looked around the new café. The sundry and bookshelves had just been installed on Monday, and painted. The counter, grills, and bar chairs put in the day before. We were almost ready. Tomorrow night I would bring in some of the books the library had donated and stack them in the bookshelves.

I had always loved the Landers' Bakery. But, there was something *extra special* about the Enchanted Cozy Cafe.

It was warm and enveloping. The walls were made of wood logs in a traditional cabin style that arched to a high ceiling with a skylight that let in the sunlight during the day and the starlight at night – when it wasn't covered with snow of course.

There was a stone rimmed cheery fireplace, and roughhewn tables where soon people would gather to chat and eat in droves. Big picture windows let in the last of the days light showing a great view of the mountain peaks of Kissing Bridge Mountain. I could just make out people coming down the snowboard trails on Eagle's peak.

The kitchen in the new café was part of the ambiance. There was a small counter with a few bar seats where the regulars would soon sit to eat and put their two cents into what ever the chef was making.

Open concept kitchen they called it.

None of their darn business is what I called it.

I pulled out a dark IPA Vermont beer from my stash in the fridge and popped the cap off. This was going to be *my secret ingredient.* Each of the five of us girls on the team were trying out different chili, based on Grandma Izzy's recipes, *but with some new trendier additions that would be our very own creations.*

The plan was for five of us to get together tomorrow night right here at the cafe, the eve of the contest. We would try each other's chili and choose a favorite. The winner would then go on to represent the new Enchanted Cozy Café as our contest entry.

Between the five of us stellar cooks, we were sure to get a chili that would be a blue ribbon winner. I secretly hoped they would pick mine so I could gain a little cred around the place. I had tough competition with this group.

Dodie Anderson, boasted veteran experience and had taken first place at the Silver Bells Christmas Cookie Contest this year, aided by the Landers of course -so she was a sure to be a tough contender.

Summer Landers had been raised by the cooking legends so she had gourmet DNA in her blood.

Carol and Ethel had that darn magic recipe book from their mom...

But *I had been trained in France.*

After the betrayal by Lance in Paris, I couldn't come straight home to face the unpleasant music. I needed time. So I sold my engagement ring, *thankfully that wasn't a fake*, and took a French cooking class with the money.

I was drunk through most of it, but I learned two things in my French cooking class that are the most important things to know about being a true gourmet chef - how to add liquor to everything you make so it tastes *'chic'*, and how to be rude to customers who asked about the makings of said *chic dish*.

That's another reason I got the job at the café – my French cooking skills. Wink wink. Actually I only had the *French liquor skill* to work with here in Kissing Bridge.

Rude didn't fly on Kissing Bridge Mountain.

Everyone was just too nice.

They didn't understand the *chicness* of being rude. Kissing Bridge Mountain is a place where people actually care about you and they take the time to say hello, plus they're all pretty much Christmas crazy all year long. That, and skiing and snowboarding. Actually, anything done in the snow, because Kissing Bridge EXCELS at snow.

Tonight I was trying out my third different chili recipe from Grandma Izzy's recipe book – this one was *You're Gonna Love it Chili*. A little on the nose, but I liked it. Plus I was going to add my dark Vermont home brew IPA that Earl up at the lodge had brewed himself. I think I had the winning combination and I was eager to get cooking.

I also kind of liked the privacy of being alone after what I'd been through. Even though I'm extremely popular – *just ask anyone* - I found out that I actually enjoyed the solace of cooking and baking. Making a great dish is so unlike life. Life just spits out whatever it wants at you like a kid that hates his peas. Splat on the plate. But, baking you could rely on. In baking you could put in all the ingredients you were supposed to, and you could pretty much count on what would come out of the darn oven.

CHAPTER 5

S peaking of ovens, I jumped when the alarm went off reminding me that the cheese muffins I was making to go with the chili were done. I opened the oven, and basked in the smell of the fresh melted cheddar and tart tarragon spice I had ground into it. I took a spatula, and lifted a corner of one to make sure it was the perfect shade of tan done. It needed just another minute.

I pushed the tray back in, when the front door of the cafe swung open with a load bang and a little bell tingle. I lifted my head quickly and banged it on the top of the shelf. Ouch. Darn Aphrodite what had she gotten herself into? I was prepared to call her out, when a group of loud people bustled into the cafe, and they were all arguing. The only one I knew was Jackson Jennings.

Jackson was my boss Carol Landers' ex fiancé. He was a short man with a shock of bright white hair that stood up a good three inches like he had seen something that made him afraid. He had the kind of eyes that were so slit you couldn't tell the color or if they were really focused on you. He was wearing a bright green suit that was expensive, but obviously bought when he was much thinner, because his gut pushed at the buttons like it wanted to break free. Despite his bad style, *initially* my heart went out to Jackson.

He wasn't particularly liked around Kissing Bridge, but I had heard the rumors of Carol Landers leaving him at the altar. I related to his heartbreak having recently endured a similar catastrophe in my own love life.

I started to say we weren't open yet, when I was cut off rudely. Any heart connection I may have felt that bonded the two of us was gone the minute Jackson Jennings opened his mouth.

"Where's Carol?" He barked angrily.

He stomped around the café like he owned it pulling his "date" with him. He dragged her around with him by her hand like she was a little poodle that wouldn't listen.

The *Poodle* wasn't from Kissing Bridge; I didn't recognize her and I knew just about everyone on the mountain. She looked like the little girl in Beatle Juice with too white a face and too dark of hair. She seemed to be about twenty-two, and as if she needed a pastry to fatten her up. I wondered what she was doing with a man old enough to be her grandpa?

"Carol!" Jackson screamed again loudly for some reason despite the whole place was pretty tiny, and she obviously wasn't there.

"Carol." He looked behind the fireplace and inside the

grate. He dug around the flames with the iron poker as if the senior was hiding there between the logs.

I rolled my eyes.

He continued searching around the one room café chanting like a madman. "Carol. Carol!"

As odd as he was acting, I found myself focused on the *huge* diamond on the Poodle's hand. Was that an engagement ring? Was Jackson engaged to the Poodle?

After making his way through every corner of the café, Jackson finally walked over to the counter and picked up the crockpot which was half full of my ingredients, still looking for Carol as if she might have shrunken up and decided to sit beneath it.

I snatched the crockpot back from him and looked at him sternly. *No one* touched Carol's crockpot unless directed. This guy was looking for trouble.

"Jackson Jennings get your hands off my boss's

crockpot! Carol's not here – and the café is not officially open yet!"

I pointed to the CLOSED sign on the door. "Any other time I'd let you look around, but I've got serious business here to get to, and we're closed. Sorry."

A whining moan like a dying hyena filled the room. I stiffened at the eerie sound. It was coming from the young man wearing a Harvard sweatshirt, and tight blue jeans, topped off with a blue parka. He was standing next to an older lady. His hair hung limply and was a dishwater-blonde and disheveled under his snowcap. He had his lip stuck out so far from pouting I couldn't tell if he had a hair lip or just a horrible attitude.

The mouth unfurled and demanded in a low long whiiiiiiiiiiiiine,"I'm hungry Uncle Jackson! You said there was food here!"

The mouth appeared to work fine.

Bad attitude it was.

He turned to the other lady, who appeared to be his mother with the same lifeless blue eyes and limp hair. She was dressed in all black with a single strand of pearls.

"I told you we shouldn't have come here mom. He's never going to change."

The mother snorted in Jackson's direction. "Gosh darn it Jackson do you have to be such a pompous arse always thinking about yourself? Let's go someplace else the young lady said they're not open and Frankie needs to eat or..."

Jackson snarled at her. "Why did you even come to Kissing Bridge? You're just here hoping I'll croak soon so you can steal my money."

The dish-washy mother's white cheeks flamed a radish purple hue, and her face pinched up like the bottom of a fig. "You mean the money you stole from us!"

She curled her elegant hands up into little balls and they shook with fury at her side. She eyed Jackson up like he was scum, and I wondered if she was going to hit Jackson right in the face.

Then they all started yelling at once.

Bratty teenager guy started banging his hands on the counter to get his hunger needs across more dramatically, and I had to stop him right there. This counter was BRAND NEW. I had seen Dan Weathers come in just yesterday and put it in himself. Quartz is expensive. FYI.

"STOP!" I had to yell to get their attention. But they ignored me.

They were all arguing again, even the Poodle was barking out something. Good grief didn't they understand I was trying to concoct our future blue ribbon winning chili? No respect.

"Hey guys!" I pleaded, "Look, I'm sorry but you all have to go. I'm cooking. As I said, this is important."

I pointed to the obvious crockpot, and the onions and chilies ready for browning in the saucepan, and then gasped, as I smelled my cheese muffins over-baking.

I pulled out the tray of burnt muffins, and tossed the hot rack on the back shelf to cool. I threw my arms up in the air exasperated. "Now I've burned my muffins!"

Bratty Harvard guy opened his mouth to protest again, I'm pretty sure he was going to repeat his complaints about being hungry again, but he must have seen the evil look in my eye and backed off.

Just in case they didn't realize the headspace I was in, I brandished my spatula to bring home the point.

"You!" I pointed to Jackson who was the leader of this idiot entourage.

He looked at me with wide eyes, but he stopped yelling. Poodle chick broke away from his slimy old man grasp and she slipped outside the door and lit a cigarette. I tried to calm myself and be professional, but I didn't put my spatula down.

"Jackson, I will tell my boss, *Carol,* that you were looking for her when I see her tomorrow. My guess is she is home with her HUSBAND – Dr. Archibald."

I pointed at the other two, and said through grated teeth, "We are not open on this side yet, but you can go next door to the Landers' Bakery side and they will *gladly serve you food.*"

Oooh how I wanted to throw in some of my trained French rudeness right now! But I refrained. I resorted to aggressively waving my spatula around again just for effect. I must have looked imposing enough because they all stopped their nonsense and looked at each other.

The fig-faced lady made a haughty gesture and said disdainfully, "The front door was open, you shouldn't keep the door unlocked if you're not open - everyone knows that."

Her stupid son nodded in agreement. "Yeah everyone knows that."

Oooh what I wanted to say.

What I did *instead*, was point wordlessly, once more, with even *bigger strokes* with my spatula, towards the door with the CLOSED sign on it.

They complained amongst themselves for another minute, and then finally grumbled their way out the front door.

When I heard it shut, I breathed a sigh of relief.

I instinctively reached for the bottle cap from the beer I had used to flavor the now burnt muffins. I felt the cool hard ridges of the cylindrical steel cap roll around in my hands, and wrapped my fingers around it lovingly. With one perfect motion, I snapped the cap with perfect precision, and a bit of annoyance, and it flew out of my hand like a bullet.

The silver bottle cap zipped across the room, banked off the bookcase, and flicked the lock mechanism on the front door to the lock position with a defiant click.

Closed, like I said.

CHAPTER 6

I locked up the café, and started home around nine o'clock. It was an extra cold night even for Kissing Bridge, and I lamented the loss of my wheels and the fact that I was back where I started.

I walked along the main street, and then turned off on Oak Ridge where I lived. The wind was blowing a weird ominous howl through the bare branches as I continued walking home in the dark cold night with Aphrodite clinging to my neck. Somehow I felt protected by her little white furry body, though I'm not sure *attack cat* is how I would describe her.

More *wuss.*

Maybe if you could attack with an irritating meow.

I wondered why I was thinking I needed protection? I did feel a strange sense of dread that was pretty unusual. Kissing Bridge was as safe a place as Mayberry RFD. I had walked these streets alone late at night without a thought since I was a young girl. Maybe it was the odd interaction with Jackson Jennings and his strange entourage? And why was he looking for Carol

Landers? Maybe he still nursed a love for her deep inside. And that weird phone call with Mr. Maritime...

CHAPTER 7

I got home to find my dad asleep on the couch with *The Voice* on TV. I swear that shows goes on for four hours straight. No telling how long he had had it on. He was still in is work uniform, and Athena was curled up on his stomach sleeping. Every time Dad breathed hard her little kitty body rose up with it.

Athena is a cool cat. She's black with large green eyes, and like her name she's definitely the smartest of the group. If they're getting in trouble I can blame it on Athena. She's also figured out Dad is the biggest softie.

I covered Dad up with a blanket, and tucked it around Athena with a quick pet. I turned off the TV just as Hera came sauntering down the stairs like the queen she is.

Hera is gray, she's a little bigger than her sisters, and her eyes are a hazel color. When she gets angry they turn a bright yellow, and even I leave the room. That yellow eye-thing is just *crazy*, and I have no idea what's going on in that furry head of hers', but I stay clear. She fancies herself the leader of the gang. Then don't they all.

I went into the kitchen and got down some of the homemade cat treats that Carol had made up for my girls.

Carol wore her badge as *Cat Woman* proudly. I was still warming up to the fact.

I put the treats in the toaster oven to heat them up. Dad had already fed the crew of goddesses, but I needed to make sure they weren't loving him more than me, so I always gave them special treats when I got home at night.

Artemis and Demeter came trotting out of the living room when they heard me open the fridge. They are best buddies, and hang out together all the time. Both are tabby colored orange and white; salt of the earth kitties just like their goddess names. They're also the most easy-going of Mrs. Olympus's brood, and rarely can be seen inside for they prefer running around outside, being natural huntresses. But I know enough to keep them home at night. Especially after the coyote got their mother.

I rinsed out each of their bowls and unwrapped Aphrodite from around my neck.

Now Aphrodite, she's a little devil - and stunningly beautiful as befitting her moniker. She knows it too. She's completely white, and her eyes are very blue almost to the point of violet like mine. (How dare she compete with my baby violet blues!)

I wasn't named Katherine Scarlet O'Hara for nothing.

The weird thing about Aphrodite is that she just loves to wear herself around my neck as if she's Princess Di and I'm supposed to carry her around! The darn thing insists on cleaving to my neck, so I've just given up. It wasn't easy to give in to this living fur feline mind you.

It's really kind of embarrassing to walk down the main street in your hometown with a cat on your neck.

But again, with all the rumors about Lance's and my fake marriage in Paris, maybe the live cat wearing fur thing works in my favor.

I'm thinking when somebody's walking around wearing a cat like Aphrodite right down Main Street that's a heck of a lot more interesting subject then another girl that got duped by her stupid idiot ex? Not that I'm holding any grudges as you can tell.

That said, I can't bring Aphrodite to the bakeshop or café with me officially, but that doesn't mean I listen. Especially since I've been working alone nights getting the café ready and nobody else is usually around. Plus since I have to walk to work, I can tell you she's better than a scarf against those mountain winds.

I put a treat in each of their kitty bowls and sat down at the kitchen table with a sigh. I couldn't get my mind around the ruckus that had just occurred. I wondered what Jackson Jennings wanted with Carol Landers? And who was that girl with him – his fiancée? I wondered if I should call Carol now, or maybe her sister Ethel? They were both newly married and wanted time at night with their husbands – thus why they hired me as extra help. I guessed it could wait until tomorrow. Still, I didn't like that Jackson Jennings one bit. I was glad Carol had chosen to marry Dr. Archibald instead.

All of the thoughts wrestled in my mind at once. At least with all this strangeness going on it had given me a few moments of relief from thinking about Lance.

I was taking that betrayal and loss day by day.

Doing just as my namesake Scarlet O'Hara advised, and choosing to "*Think about it tomorrow, after all tomorrow is another day...* "

With this mantra, somehow, Scarlett managed to successfully get away with never actually dealing with anything. I envied her that. By pushing every issue that bothered her off into that endless tomorrow, she never had to actually deal with it, because her tomorrows never came.

I opened the fridge and grabbed a beer, and flipped off the cap with my opener. I looked at the shiny silver ridges and wrapped my fingers around it. The bottle cap felt good in my hand. As I twirled the cool metal, it relaxed my mind. I sat for a while thinking, twirling and drinking.

I noticed it was getting late and I wanted to get up super early to go talk to the Landers.

I manipulated the bottle cap between my thumb and forefinger and then snapped it hard. It hit the back door, ricocheted off the wall shutting off the kitchen lights, and then toppled into the recycling bin next to the sink. Two points.

My cell phone rang and it startled me. It was late. I looked down to see Lance's handsome face on the screen.

Never again Lance.

CHAPTER 8

There are some men who come into your life that you can never forget. My fake newlywed ex-husband *was not one of those men.* In fact, I could barely wait to erase the memory of his lying, deceiving, and slightly paunchy butt. *Especially,* after he had the nerve to trick me into marrying him on Christmas Eve in Paris, *with a fake marriage certificate.*

Somehow, Lance, *my ex,* had reasoned that the formality of legality didn't matter when it came to the exchange of my long held and overrated virginity.

Tell that to Saint Anthony.

That said, there was no bringing it back now.

When I found out the falsehood that Lance had put together to fool me, I was outraged. How could he have done that to me after all we had been through together? It was a betrayal on the highest level. Literally, he planned a whole fake marriage ceremony that didn't count? A new low even for him.

For sure I had been surprised when he flew out to meet me with his sudden wedding plans, especially after all the time I had waited for him. (We'd been in a long distance relationship for two long years.)

The ceremony in Paris had been magic, and a big huge lie.

It made *no sense* to me why he would concoct such a charade!

At first, I just didn't know how I could return to my hometown of Kissing Bridge with the news. I had already told my dad we were married, and goodness knows the pub news spreads fast on the mountain! Now I had to go home and explain why I was still single – officially – yet tarnished, nonetheless.

Good grief. I just prayed my father wouldn't ask for details. I had enough Catholic guilt of my own to work on denying without my dad chiming in with his. I would never forgive Lance, and I wasn't about to answer his phone calls.

CHAPTER 9

I came into work early the next day to talk to Ethel and Carol in person about the weird actions of Carol's ex beau last night.

Dodie Anderson was at the counter ringing up sales. Dodie is a sweetheart, not a bad bone in her body. She's a pretty girl with a china doll face and big blue eyes, and she is the day manager that oversees the bakery. On top of overseeing the bakery, she teaches the cooking class on Saturday mornings.

Dodie was a newcomer to the mountain, having recently moved to Kissing Bridge, but after working at the Landers Bakery she knew everyone in town by their first name. Right now she was commandeering the busy front counter with expertise, while passing orders off to the back kitchen.

The place was buzzing as usual. People just couldn't get enough of the Landers' baked goods. I waved to Dodie as I slid past her and into the back kitchen.

"Morning everyone," I said to the crew as I continued on past the myriad of ovens and bakers all dressed in white.

I found the infamous Landers sisters in the back of the bakery, both of them hands deep in dough and chatting away happily. I had to smile at the sight of them deep at work like Da Vinci and Michelangelo.

Carol was well over seventy, but still a force of nature. She was tall and regal and still beautiful for her age. Carol wore her ruby red hair in an epic sized beehive. Her flaming hairdo raised a good two feet in the air, making her resemble a red haired version of Marge Simpson.

Beside her stood her younger sister, Ethel. She was a lovely senior as well. She had ethereal blonde, nearly white hair that usually fell softly to her shoulders, but was currently tucked into a neat bun. She was slight, and petite, with the prettiest soft blue eyes. She appeared very demure, but she wasn't one bit.

The Landers ladies were also about as celebrity as it got in Kissing Bridge.

Due to their family lineage, and their mother Izzy's infamous recipe book – some said "*spell book*" – the Landers ladies had managed to win the Christmas Eve Silver Bells Cookie Contest for the last seventy years.

Many believed that their mother Izzy's recipes held a kind of magic to the one that ingested it. Certainly the Landers baked goods had charmed the residents of

Kissing Bridge for decades.

Upon getting to know the sisters more intimately, I discovered that cooking and baking *were not* the Landers only gifts.

The entire Landers family had talents that most of the town didn't know about.

Unbeknownst to most of the small town of Kissing Bridge Mountain, *where people prided themselves on knowing everything about everyone,* the rumors of magical tendencies in the Landers' family were - *completely true.*

After being in the dining room and asking Ethel a question about a certain pastry, and having Carol answer that question from *the kitchen* –

I had learned that Carol Landers *actually had some kind of superman hearing skills* - like the six million dollar man.

Ethel confessed that her sister Carol was born with the innate ability to eavesdrop on conversations from across a crowded noisy room with a 99% accuracy. Despite the fact that you couldn't miss Carol's presence in any room, with that tower high flaming hair, one would never suspect she could hear every word you said from a football field length away.

Gee, that was comforting to know as an employee.

Ethel Landers was bequeathed with rare gifts of her own. For one, she had a unique gift for color. Not only did this trait translate into a wonderful style sense, it also spilled over into near detective-like qualities of minor hue differences. Her many culinary wins as the cookie Queen could be attributed, partially, to that color talent. On top of that, Ethel had more energy than a teenager despite her being in her seventies.

Between you and me, I'm pretty sure she might have some Dorian Gray painting hanging around her attic some-where.

Then there was Summer, Ethel's daughter, and former supermodel. No one quite knew what her gift was, other than a lucky seating talent, and a face to die for. Maybe that was enough for one person.

But there had been rumors about her cat....

Despite things being really messed up in my personal life, at least I had a good crew of women friends at work.

That can cure a heck of a lot.

I missed my mom. And somehow the Landers ladies filled a void in me. I felt like part of a family again working with them. A kitchen can be a warzone and you make combat buddies fast and hard during a lunch rush at the height of ski season.

I got straight to the point because I have no tact.

"Hey Carol, Jackson came into the café yesterday with a group of weirdos I've never seen. He acted like he was going to die if he didn't see you. I didn't want to call and bother you at home and he seemed a little cray cray." I made the "he's loco" motion next to my head.

Carol looked confused. "Why would he be looking for me?"

A big hrmmph came out of her sister Ethel, and she made dramatic motions as she removed her plastic gloves covered with flour. "We're banning him from the new café Carol. I don't want him in our new place he's bad mojo!"

Not that anyone asked me, but I agreed with Ethel.

"Well I don't know what he wanted, but he was pretty serious about finding you. Can't say he is a very nice person. He was mean to his sister, and I guess she came all the way here to Kissing Bridge with her son just to visit. They had a big fight about money."

Carol's dark brows rose in unison. "Sister? Well they haven't spoken in years...I wonder what brings her here to Kissing Bridge? And with her son as well – Frankie I think it is..."

I shrugged. "It was a pretty weird day. One thing for sure is people are pretty anxious for us to open."

I thought about Mr. Maritime hanging around out front as well.

Ethel waltzed over to the sink to wash her hands. "Thankfully we seem to be right on schedule. I see the new crockpots came in?"

I nodded. "Yep. We're going to be the most colorful crew at the contest."

"As planned." Ethel tossed over her shoulder as she finished drying her hands.

Carol seemed to be captivated by something in her dough bowl.

"Anyway, I'll see you all later tonight to pick out our chili see which one of us has the best entrée for the contest!"

Ethel winked at me.

She was psyched. I knew she had been secretly working on her chili recipe up at the lodge kitchen so we wouldn't know what she was up to.

I was watching that Ethel.

I was pretty confident my special chili version would be the best, but I'd be foolish to count out any of the

Landers.

I eyed Ethel up suspiciously.

My secret dark beer-infused chili can take her, I thought.

Ethel, you're going down.

CHAPTER 10

The Six Pines Valley Chili Cook-Off was the biggest crockpot chili show down south of Burlington.

Bakers, chefs, and homegrown chili experts gathered from all over Vermont to compete for the blue ribbon.

By winning the big deal Six Pines Valley Chili Cook-Off, we all hoped to make our mark on the lower foothills of Kissing Bridge Mountain and advertise the grand opening of the Enchanted Cozy Cafe.

We had cards and coupons printed up, and obviously the best chili in the contest. Our goal was to fill the new cafe with new customers willing to take the jaunt up the mountain for some cozy comfort food which we specialized in. We were already a hit with our hometown, but here at the contest we hoped to lure in a whole new fan base.

Six Pines Valley was just down the mountain from

Kissing Bridge. Its streets were narrow and there were chimneys in every home, but whereas Kissing Bridge was always kissed with snow, Six Pines got the rain.

Tonight a storm lashed out over Six Pines. The pine trees that dotted the main center swayed in the heavy winds, and rain pelted down in sheets so hard it hurt. The dour climate outside, however, was the exact opposite of the warm and welcoming party of chili lovers inside the town pavilion center gym.

The center was packed with locals, and many of the inhabitants of Kissing Bridge who had made the trek to support the Landers' new endeavor. There must have been three hundred people altogether.

Upon entry into the pavilion, each person was given a little golden spoon, and a red paper bracelet to show they had paid to get in. The golden spoon allowed you to taste any of the wonderful chili samples that were being passed out by the contestants.

I had learned about wine in Paris, *(by learning I mean drank a lot of it)* and I can tell you no vino can beat good old Vermont mountain home brewed beer – *especially* when it came to making homemade finger licking good chili. And that deep dark specialty beer *was our secret ingredient.*

Thanks to Earl Elkins' homebrew, added to Grandma

Izzy's original smoke–*infused,* long hour simmered crockpot concoction recipe –*my chili* had been chosen to represent the Enchanted Cozy Café!!!

I told you about that French liquor thing being the magical dove up my sleeve.

We were so packed at our booth we could barely keep up. We were passing out cards and coupons left and right. I was certain we had the lock on the blue ribbon. After all, the chili was based around Grandma Izzy Landers' original recipe I had just perked up a bit - so we kind of had the win in the bag.

I did mention the magic right?

Ethel, Carol, Dodie, Summer, and I donned matching uniforms, as did every team competing. We wore jeans, and our tiffany blue t-shirts emblazoned with the *Enchanted Cozy Café* in shiny silver thread. All in all we had five crockpots bubbling at our table, and a crowd of chili lovers pushing through to get our samples.

The crowd at the Six Pines Valley Chili Cook-Off was LOVING US!

I couldn't help but smile. This was turning out to be a good time, and it looked like we were the crowd favorite.

When one of the judges waddled up to try a sample and I saw the look of love on his face – I knew we were going to win.

It was six o'clock and the contest would be over in an hour. We were serving up our chili so fast we could barely keep up.

I noticed Jackson Jennings pushing up to our booth with his weirdo goth attired girlfriend *-the Poodle.*

His face was redder than usual. I had heard he had a house here in Six Pines but I hadn't expected to see him tonight. He was aggressively shoving people away from our booth, as he made his way toward the front where Aunt Carol was stationed, all the while still tugging the skinny girl.

He finally broke his way to the front of the booth, and demanded a sample, all the while eyeing up Carol. I had heard from Ethel that Jackson was used to getting his way because he had about as much money as God.

Oil man.

Rumor was he'd gotten lucky and found oil under his old family homestead. His money made him cantankerous and he was already pretty unlikeable. He had what I refer to as 'resting b.... face. Even relaxed his face made an angry look like he had smelled something bad.

He had that kind of face.

People in Kissing Bridge were kind, so everyone was nice to him, but only Earl really got along with him and that was based more on their love of good cigars and tough ski runs.

Ethel made a face at Jackson as she slid out from behind our booth. "Watch my pot for me darling," She whispered, "I have to run quick and visit the powder room."

I nodded. "I got it Ethel."

Jackson was making a complete spectacle of himself trying to get Carol to notice him. The cantankerous octogenarian, with his bright white hair, was screaming and making a circus of himself waving a fifty dollar bill around Carol's crockpot and yelling, "What's it take to get some service around here?"

Humph. I'd give him service all right...

But Carol didn't have time for her old wandering beau, and she ignored his attempts to get her attention with his money waving bloviating self.

She was too busy for his antics.

Winning the chili cook-off was serious business.

I looked at the masses of chili lovers hovering around our table with gleeful faces. At this rate we would run out of chili before the contest was over, and that wouldn't leave a good taste in the judges' mouth.

I thought it was time to alert Aunt Carol that we better get the backup crock pots from the van, and start warming them up because we needed to get some more chili going.

The Landers always kept *backups* for everything, because they'd been around long enough to know stuff happens in baking.

Carol was barking out orders to us girls behind the booth like Patton to his troops. I abandoned my crockpot post, and hastened over to explain our dilemma to the General.

"We're all running low. We need the backups crockpots of chili in the van." I said breathlessly.

Carol's alert blue eyes darted down the line of crockpots taking in the dilemma of the dwindling chili supplies. Summer and Dodie were spooning up samples from their colored crockpots as quick as they could. All the pots were nearly empty.

Carol nodded with a sharp curt movement that made her large red beehive tilt over like the tower of Pisa. "I'm on it. Tell Ethel to follow me when you she comes back from the bathroom, I can't carry all three of them and I need you here to fend off the over zealous chili eaters. Summer's too much of a softie. One to a customer *that's it,* got it?"

"Got it."

With that she grabbed her coat and sped towards the back door of the pavilion center. I stood on my tiptoes attempting to spot Ethel over the crowd as more and more people swarmed into our booth for more of our chili.

All of the Enchanted Cozy Café coupons had been snatched up as well. It certainly seemed like the word about the upcoming grand opening had gotten out!

I could see our popularity was not lost on the contest judges who kept staring over at the masses around our table. It seemed certain that the Landers were going to be taking home another culinary blue ribbon – *crockpot chili style.*

Obviously, then, I wasn't at all surprised that we made the finalists in the Six Pines Valley Chili Cook- Off contest.

But the whole *murder thing…*

Well, I never saw that coming.

CHAPTER 11

We'd been waiting ten minutes and neither of the Lander sisters had shown up with the backup crockpots.

I told the girls I better go check the van. Maybe they needed help.

Dodie moved over to Ethel's pot and Summer switched over to Carol's. I poked my head out the back door trying to spot Ethel or Aunt Carol. There was the van, but no seniors.

I went back inside, and muscled my way through the crowd towards the powder room.

They weren't there either.

I made my way to the front door of the pavilion center. Earl Elkins, lean and tall like an old Marlboro man, and newly married to Ethel Landers, stood outside the front door staring at the sky and looking about aimlessly. Maybe he was wondering where Ethel was too?

I called out to him through the door. "Earl! Hey Earl!"

His piercing grey eyes turned as he heard his name float

over the wind. I waved. He waved back. The rain had stopped a moment, and his breath came out in frozen clouds.

I yelled to him from the door. "Earl, have you seen Carol or Ethel? We need those backup crockpots with the chili now!"

Earl looked concerned. He took a step towards me."No, I was just out here talking to Jackson and he just went to grab a Cuban cigar to –"

He looked off down the way presumably towards Jackson's house and then walked up to me. He shivered a bit and shook off his jacket. "What did you say? You need something out of the van?"

I nodded and explained about the backup crockpots and how we were running out of chili, and I didn't have the keys for the van. He was a good six foot four inches tall so he scanned the packed room from above like an eagle scouting for the two sisters.

"There's Ethel!" He pointed towards the judges' table. The thin Spanish looking judge had Ethel deep in conversation. Ethel kept looking over her shoulder. She knew we were nearing the finish line, but she obviously couldn't be rude to one of the judges and just walk away.

I grabbed Earl.

"Go save your wife and get those backup crockpots or we're doomed! Carol says the last moments before the contest judging are the most crucial. People tend to remember the most recent chili they tasted. Go!"

Earl was smart enough not to question anything regarding cooking and the Landers. He hastened his way through the crowd. "Excuse me. Pardon me. Hello Cyrus nice to see you. Excuse me."

Thank goodness for Earl, he was going to get Ethel and meet Carol to help with the backups and protect our potential blue medal ribbon!

CHAPTER 12

The tension at the chili cook-off was getting to me. Since I *officially* didn't have anything to do before they returned with the backup chili and crockpots – I slipped out the front door for a quick cigarette.

The rain started again as soon as I walked outside. Darn the weather in Six Pines! But I was desperate. I found a little awning at the end of the building under the gutter where it kind of protected me from the rain.

I lit up a cigarette, and looked up at the moonless night. It was really raining extra hard now, and water kept rolling off the awning and hitting me in my face.

I wiped at my eyes with my free hand. I lamented that I didn't have my coat on. Did I mention I was *sneaking a smoke*? One of the disadvantages of smoking that the French don't have to endure. They're civilized. They accept second hand smoke as a part of growing up *chic*.

Chic or not, my father's ire would be worse than my current goosebumps and wet hair too if I got caught.

Suddenly, through the mist, I spotted a figure bent over, and huddled next to a large green Victorian home a few door down. It was a strange position for someone to be in, and why would anyone be out in this rain - other than a crazy smoker like me?

I craned my neck to see better.

My eyesight is not great, and the drenching down rain was making it even harder to see what was going on.

The person was certainly hunched over in an odd position.

Maybe he was throwing up from some of the competitor's chili? Goodness knows I almost burped right in front of the team from Deep River Run. Granted, I had been drinking beer. But I always drank beer.

The huddled figure suddenly bolted up straight, and looked right at me. He turned his head in each direction and then moved towards me down the street. I was glad he was all right.

From inside, the announcer's amplified voice said, "Everyone please quiet down! The official semifinalists are about to be announced!"

Shoot!

I had to get in there now! I stubbed out my cigarette, and rushed toward the door.

A weird sensation rushed through me, and from out of the corner of my eye I turned to see the dark figure running in my direction. I thought he must have wanted to get into the pavilion to hear the semi finalist announcements too.

That's when I saw the knife in his hand.

I looked around to see if there was some animal about to attack or something, but we were alone outside. Even the darn alley cats were in the pavilion waiting on the contestant announcement, and scraps of course.

Surely he wasn't coming after me? I'm not what you would call a smart person, but I had a feeling I might be in danger. By the time my Einstein brain figured that out, the figure was almost upon me. Large, dressed in black with a really big knife. BIG. Like - *carve the turkey on Christmas big.* The front door was close and there were hundreds of people inside but no one here to save me.

He was closing in on me fast.

I blinked out of my temporary shock, and I reached in my back jeans pocket without thinking, and fired off a beer bottle cap right at my oncoming assailant. He yelped and stopped, not sure what he'd been hit with. That's all the break I needed to jet back into the pavilion, and the safety of the crowd.

I ran through the front door and into the loud busy melee. I pushed my way through the crowd towards our booth, instinctively weaving back and forth through the throng like I'd seen in the crime movies. Only I think they weave when they're being shot at.

I didn't know what was going on.

I didn't know if that was even a real knife or some stunt. All I knew was that I didn't have time to deal with this lunatic now. I was slightly drunk and full of chili and they were ringing the bell to make the official winner's announcement.

I made my way back to our booth in the corner, panting and breathless. I looked back through the crowd, but the lunatic hadn't followed me in through the door. Was he still outside somewhere lurking? Why had he come after me? I had so many questions but my head was spinning. I was so discombobulated I ran straight into Earl Elkins and almost knocked myself out.

"You okay Kat?" Earl peered down at me with concern. I shook off the stars out of my head, and hustled to take my place next to the rest of the girls in our line of crockpots. I didn't know what had just happened.

"Yes – no - I don't think so. I think we need to call the police, there's a lunatic out there and he chased me for some reason! Earl he had a knife!"

Earl's eyes went wide. "I'm going to find Jaime. He just got off duty – I saw him come in. I'll be back. Stay inside."

I saw Jaime across the way talking to Mr. Maritime and his wife. Jaime Henderson looked like a California surfer more than a Kissing Bridge cop. I couldn't get used to thinking of Jaime as a law enforcer, since we spent so much time breaking rules together growing up. We had dated in high school but I hadn't seen him since I'd gotten back to Kissing Bridge. His parents owned the Wine and Cheese shop– *Wino's* – right across from the Landers' Bakery in main town. I knew he still helped around their store, but I had yet to run into him. I breathed a sigh of relief as I saw Earl pull him aside and point out the door.

The announcer rang a cowbell to quiet the crowd.

All of us girls were lined up in the booth awaiting the results. Summer smiled her super watt smile and shot me the thumbs up as I took my place in line with the team. I was glad she felt confident, and that the extra crockpots had made it to the booth where people were still stopping by for samples despite the contest being officially over.

I looked down at the red Sears crockpot I had ordered for Aunt Carol standing solitary at the end of the table.

There was Aunt Carol's red contest crockpot.

But where was Aunt Carol?

CHAPTER 13

The fourth, fifth, and sixth place winners received certificates, handshakes, and photos with the judges, but no ribbons. Those were reserved for the top three coveted spots that would take home the yellow, red and blue ribbons.

It was almost seven o'clock; any moment they would announce the top three awards for the Six Pines Chili Cook-Off. By all accounts it looked like our Enchanted Cozy Café Chili was a shoe in for the blue ribbon. Luckily we had those spares because Dodie said the crowd was on that chili as soon as they had it plugged in. I made small talk, while a knot formed in my stomach.

Carol's personal old red crockpot was the *biggest crockpot*, and held the most chili. And she had left before any of us to go get it – why wasn't she back yet? And why hadn't Earl and Ethel gone to fetch all three instead of just the two?

I brought my hand to my heart. The head judge took the microphone once more.

"And now for the top three ribbon winners..."

This was the moment we had all been waiting for. Aunt Carol wouldn't miss this if she had a breath of life in her.

I felt a chill go up my spine despite the heat of the chili fumes.

CHAPTER 14

C arol never showed.

Summer Landers was next to me with her bright yellow crockpot. She still had a crowd around her despite the fact she had no chili left in her crockpot. Most of the townies wanted her autograph (she was a Sports Illustrated bathing suit model after all) and she had happily scribbled them out on the back of the new Enchanted Cozy Café cards we had printed. With her autograph on it they wouldn't be tossing those café business cards away for certain. She smiled her mega watt-blinding bulb of teeth and people just melted. Right now I needed her to watch my chili.

"Summer" I whispered to her, "can you give out the rest of my samples I have to go look for your aunt – have you seen her?"

Summer shook her head, but a thought flitted across her beautiful face. "Some big guy gave me a note for her a while ago but I haven't seen her since."

"Note? What kind of note?"

Summer lifted her shoulders. "I don't know except it was

definitely from Jackson."

My eyebrows lifted at this news. "How do you know it was from Jackson?"

"Oh Jackson uses this swanky red wax insignia with his initials in it. He puts it on all of his correspondences."

Hmmm. This was odd. Why would Carol's ex beau be slipping her secret notes at the chili Cook-Off? Especially when he was here with another woman – his Poodle fiancée? My spidey sense went off. I yanked off my apron and Summer slid down one spot to take over serving the very last of the samples from my crockpot. I had to go find Carol.

I stepped behind Summer and I grabbed Ethel's hand. I squeezed it tight and whispered. "We're going to win."

Ethel's wise eyes darted across the judge's table and she nodded.

"I feel good about it."

I didn't want to scare her with what I was thinking. I composed myself, which is really difficult for me.

"I'm going to check for Carol in the bathroom." I lied.

Ethel was entranced in the moment, her eyes locked on the judges, awaiting our first big win together. "Uh huh." She said not really listening. "She's probably in the back kitchen washing her crockpot out you know how she is about that. Tell her to hurry dear they're about to start."

She turned to her daughter Summer. "Oh Summer I think we have a winner!"

I spotted Earl coming back in the front door with Jaime at his side. He caught my eye and shook his head and mouthed. "Gone."

I felt better knowing they looked into it.

I slipped out from behind the booth and made a beeline through the other competitor's tables and into the main kitchen. I looked around the kitchen but it was deserted. Neither Aunt Carol nor her crockpot were anywhere in sight. The judges were still drawing out announcing the major winners as they thanked everyone in the state of Vermont, and their mothers.

I rushed out of the abandoned kitchen, and pushed through the mob that had thickened near the judge's stand. It was heavy moving through the throngs. People were talking loudly and drinking too much with the excuse of dulling the chili spice.

Whether that was true or not, it made for a darn ruckus and a good party.

I needed to talk to Jaime. I felt a sense of doom. First that strange guy outside that seemed deranged, now Carol missing. I hoped they weren't related. Even if she went to talk to Jackson, she should have been back by now.

And where were Jackson, and his Poodle fiancé anyway? Maybe he could tell me where she was?

I broke through the crowd over by the judge's table and cut in on Earl and Jaime's conversation.

"Well here she is – Kat – tell Jaime what happened with that strange man. No telling if he is out to hurt someone and still about..."

I nodded emphatically. "Yes yes it was very weird. But I'm worried – Carol she should have been back with her crockpot. When you got the others from the van was her personal big red crockpot – the one with her initials in gold – was that there as well?"

Earl thought about it. "No – just the two were in the back seat. I would have grabbed the extra crockpot if I spotted it. Ethel and I figured Carol had already taken it. The door was still open to the back of the van."

I let out my breath hard. "Have you seen Jackson?"

Earl looked confused. "Not in the last fifteen minutes – he was running by his house just a few doors down to grab a Cuban cigar he had gotten and wanted to share I don't know what's holding him up..."

He looked around the room. He pointed out the goth chick over by the refreshment table – no Jackson.

"Carol and Jackson are *both* absent? Earl can you show

me, which house Jackson lives in? I think they may be there together and I need to find Carol."

Earl raised his eyebrows and sucked in his breath. The judges were lining up to announce the winner and no Carol. That was a problem.

I continued on quickly as I saw the judges all taking their seats. "Look Summer said someone gave Carol a note from Jackson – can you show me which house is his I think I better go look for her there."

Earl's skin began to whiten. "It's just down the way a couple buildings down – big green house with a wraparound porch."

I nodded. "Wish me luck."

Earl said. 'I'll go out back and check the parking lot and the van!"

I headed for the front door without thinking. Jaime's hand grabbed my shoulder.

"I'm coming with you," he said. "Just in case."

I was going to tell him I was a big girl and didn't need him, but after that weirdo chasing me I wasn't feeling so big in my britches.

I nodded. "Let's go."

CHAPTER 14

Jackson's house was less than a hundred yards away, but it seemed like a mile.

The rain was whipping so hard it was nearly blinding. No moon graced the dark night, and the howling of some cold animal, and the memory of that man with a knife filled me with dread.

Jaime and I shuffled as quickly as possible along the slippery walk trying to keep our footing. We made it to the house and started up the stairs. The house was old but magnificent. It had a sign out front with a badge proclaiming it was a historical sight that had stood since 1745.

The old wood porch creaked and groaned under our feet as we pounded up the short flight of stairs together and banged on the door. No answer.

Jaime tried the door, and it swung open eerily as if by some windy spectral hand. He called out to Jackson, but there was no reply. He tried the light switch but the power was out. I gulped.

"Jackson you here man?" Jaime called out to the dark

house.

Nothing.

Jaime flipped on his flashlight, and we made our way through the dark house gingerly.

Why would Aunt Carol be here when the contest was nearly over? Suddenly, a window blew open hard, hitting the wall behind it, and sending glass shattering around our feet. I jumped back surprised, and that's when we heard the startled scream from the kitchen.

Jaime drew his gun and motioned for me to stay back.

Of course I didn't.

I followed him into the kitchen, albeit behind him. The kitchen was dim, and there were cupboards flung open, and things thrown about in an odd disarray. The floor creaked under our feet as we made our way slowly into the kitchen.

Jaime called out, "Ms. Landers? Jackson? Anyone here?"

Suddenly, he stopped, and put up a hand to stop me from seeing, but it was too late.

There splayed out on the old wooden kitchen floor was the motionless body of Jackson Jennings. He was lying on his back with his rain boots still on, and there was a stream of blood running from the side of his head. His small motionless frame was afloat in a sea of chili and his shock of white hair had bits of what looked like carrot stuck to it.

At the foot of the dead body was Aunt Carol.

CHAPTER 15

A unt Carol had her signature red crockpot in her hands, and her mouth appeared stuck in a perpetual "O" with no sound coming out.

There was a distinct red blood blotch running from the top of the crockpot as she held it up in front of her as if she was frozen.

I clapped my hand to my mouth. I had never seen a dead body before but Jackson Jennings sure looked dead. Jaime ran over to him and checked his pulse. He took in the wound on the side of his head and the pile of chili he was laying in. He looked at me and shook his head confirming my fear.

This was horrible, how had Carol been dragged into this? I wondered if Jackson had a heart attack or maybe slipped in the chili? What an ugly way to go. Poor Carol...

I went to hug her when I heard a deep voice growl, "Hands up. Don't move. Put the crockpot down lady."

I put my hands up in the air, but Aunt Carol stood frozen with a death grip on her crockpot staring at it as if it had grown wings. A Six Pines Deputy came in with his gun drawn and his cuffs out. I recognized him right away – it was Det. Fuzzbottom. He brushed by Jamie and me without a glance and barked at Carol.

"Hand over the crockpot lady before I have to get rough with you."

Carol seemed to blink back to life as she looked at the scene around her in bewilderment. She handed the deputy the crockpot and looked back at Jackson's body. She began to tremble. "Oh no – is he, is he...."

"DEAD," Fuzzbottom said dully. "And by the looks of the blood on this crockpot I'd say this is the murder weapon. Put your hands behind your back Ms. Landers. You're under arrest for the murder of Jackson Jennings."

CHAPTER 16

Fuzzbottom yanked the crockpot out of Carol's hands and slammed it on the table. Then he turned to Jaime. "You local?" he said.

"Kissing Bridge deputy..." Jaime said. He glanced at Carol.

Fuzzbottom slapped the cuffs on Carol. He tossed his head in the direction of the crockpot. "Put that into evidence – don't touch it. I don't know how you Kissing Bridge people do things."

Jaime's mouth tightened. He disappeared out the front door and returned a few moments later with a pair of gloves from his patrol car in the parking lot. He lifted up the bloodied crockpot carefully, and put it into plastic wrap for evidence and finger printing.

Carol's shoulders were rigid and she didn't even move to blink as the cop pushed her towards the front door. Anger heated my blood watching that Det. Fuzzbottom with his seedy aviator sunglasses on even at night. Even if he did think she murdered Jackson, which I'm sure she didn't, that was no way to treat a lady old enough to be his grandmother. Hairy loser.

He shoved Carol harder towards the door. She looked at me blankly and said, "I just picked it up off the floor, I didn't even see him until…Oh Kat it was horrible. The note said he had my crockpot and it was a matter of life and death."

Fuzzbottom was having none of it. "Tell it to the judge lady." He pushed her forward and down the wet stairs.

I would have cried, but Carol didn't. I'm a big baby that way. Most likely she was still in shock. I guess the act of seeing your ex dead in a pool of blue ribbon winning chili (Yes we won) was just too much for anyone to take.

I followed behind her trying to give her encouragement. "I'll call Dr. Archibald as soon as I get back to the contest."

Carol's voice was shaky as Fuzzbottom pushed her into the back of his cop car. "He's at the hospital. Tell him what happened won't you Kat?"

I nodded in sympathy, and fought back the tears that filled my eyes.

It was horrible seeing her in the back of the cop car with her bright red beehive smooshed down around her because it was too high for the car roof. She looked like a sad Ronald McDonald doll with her pale face and weird bouffant hair squished down around her. Of course Ronald never had handcuffs on, or was accused of murder with an egg McMuffin.

Or in Carol's case – having croaked a guy with a crockpot.

CHAPTER 17

Of course we won the 1st place at the chili contest, but it wasn't excitement that got me up early the next morning. Carol Landers was innocent and it was up to us at the bakery to prove it.

I knew Ethel would be opening up the bakery at 6 AM. I had some time to think about this, and we had to figure out a way to get Aunt Carol out of jail. I knew she was innocent.

I had seen somebody in the bushes right by Jackson's house, that same somebody that came running towards me – that same somebody that should have a nick from my bottle cap somewhere on their body.

A CLOSED sign hung at the front of the Landers' Bakery door even though I knew Ethel was there. Her car – and Dodie's for that matter – was parked on the street out in front. Not very incognito if that was the point.

I knocked on the window, but nobody answered. The lights were off and it seemed lifeless. I tried Dodie on her cell first. She was the manager so she usually arrived before everyone else in the wee hours. It went to voicemail. Then I tried Ethel's cell.

She picked up and hissed in a whisper, "SHHHHHH! Come in the back door we're in the kitchen."

I looked both ways and cut between the slim alley between Max's scrapbooking shop and the new cafe. It was way too early for Maxine to be in. Her shop didn't open until 10:00 AM because she was on European time. Although she lived her entire life in Kissing Bridge she cleaved to her English lineage and lingered over tea late into the morning.

I made it to the back door, and tried the handle to the bakery, but it was locked. I knocked on the back door but there was no answer. I had no idea what Dodie and Ethel were doing. I knocked again.

Again no answer.

What were they doing? I remembered Ethel had insisted we all learn a secret knock. I tried to remember the knock. I finally just got creative to let them know that it was me and not somebody else, so I did a triple tap, double tap, and single tap – and Ethel threw open the door. She had a wild look in her eyes as she scanned the back parking lot looking both ways, and then pulled me inside.

Kat's Dark Beer Infused Blue Ribbon Winning Chili

INGREDIENTS

- 1 1/2 tablespoons ground cumin
- 2 tablespoons of ground cinnamon
- 1 tablespoon ground coriander
- 5 pounds ground chuck
- 2 tablespoons canola oil
- 2 1/2 pounds onions, coarsely chopped
- 1 1/2 pounds red bell peppers, seeded, cut into 1/2-inch pieces
- 1 1/2 pounds yellow bell peppers, seeded, cut into 1/2-inch pieces
- 2 large jalapeño chilies with seeds, chopped (about 1/3 cup)
- 7 tablespoons chili powder
- 2 teaspoons (packed) minced canned chipotle chilies in adobo sauce*
- 2 28-ounce cans crushed tomatoes with added puree
- 2 15-ounce cans kidney beans, drained
- 1 12-ounce bottle dark beer (such as stout or a

good Vermont IPA)

- Sour cream

- Chopped green onions

- Coarsely grated extra-sharp cheddar cheese

RECIPE PREPARATION

- Toast cumin and coriander in skillet over medium heat until darker and beginning to smoke, about 4 minutes. Cool.

- Sauté beef in heavy large pan medium-high heat until no longer pink, breaking up with spoon. Heat oil in large skillet over medium-high heat. Add onions, all bell peppers, and jalapeños. Sauté until vegetables begin to soften, about 15 minutes. Add mixture to crockpot along with the meat. Mix in toasted spices, chili powder, and chipotle chilies. Add crushed tomatoes, beans, and beer. Let chili cook on high, stirring occasionally, for one hour. Reduce heat on the crockpot and simmer on low for two hours. Season with salt and pepper. Cool slightly. Refrigerate uncovered until cold, then cover and keep refrigerated up to 2 days (or freeze up to 1 month). Rewarm over medium-low heat.

- Ladle chili into bowls. Serve with sour cream, green onions, and cheese.

CHAPTER 18

It was a dismal site inside the back of the bakery kitchen this morning. Usually the back of Landers' Bakery was like walking into a sunny morning dream. People chatting and singing as they created the specials of the day, and every imaginable smell of comfort food wafting around you in a big aromatic hug.

But now it was empty, and most of the stoves were cold. There were no trays of pastries ready to go, no other employees at all – other than Dodie. She was drinking coffee lost in thought, when a stove buzzer rang and she got up to check it.

The Landers' Bakery might not be opening today, but that didn't stop the need for some sugar when things were tough. I liked these girls' priorities.

Dodie pulled out a fresh baked pastry tart. It shone with

a glaze of butter on its perfectly done crust and it smelled heavenly.

"What's in that?" The newfound gourmet in me just had to know.

Dodie smiled. "It's made with fresh strawberries and key lime filling."

Hmmm interesting combo. I drooled as I watched her pull out a pastry tube and drizzle warm chocolate on top.

Ethel sat back down at the small table with me and played with her chamomile tea bag dunking it in and swirling, dunking it in and swirling. I was nearly hypnotized by the swinging bag when Ethel suddenly bolted out of her seat like a rocket, and scampered around rechecking the restaurant for any possible breaches.

She made a quick dart around the room making sure all the windows were closed, and readjusted all the curtains to make sure they were pulled tight. She was extra rattled and amped up – even for Ethel. She let out a big huff, and then came back and sat back down with a serious expression. She almost looked her age as she slumped over in a defeated position and contemplated the situation before us.

Ethel is in her seventies, and most of the time she looks like a sweet elderly elegant very beautiful lady. But I've gotten to know Ethel and let me tell you, that *old lady thing is all a big charade.* Old lady –Ha! She can run faster than me. I'm not kidding. I'm not a great athlete, or even very graceful, but I am less *than half her age!* I raced against her at the fair in the thirty and over contest to win a free bottle of champagne, and she smoked me. Like she came in *way ahead of me* – it was humiliating. She beat me in the obstacle course too. Whatever, I'd had a beer.

But now, her beloved sister Carol was in jail for murder. Sure Ethel had just sharpened her amateur sleuth teeth during the recent Christmas cookie cutout recipe theft debacle – but it hadn't prepared her for the magnitude of dealing with something like this.

"We've got to put our heads together and figure out how to get Carol out of jail." I said.

Dodie set the tarts down on the table and joined us. They looked amazing. I picked one up, and took a little nibble. Hmmmm! I inspected the tart thoroughly discerning any nuances I might learn as a new chef. I glanced at Dodie from under my lashes with newfound respect.

Note to Self: Chocolate, like liquor, makes about anything taste better.

Dodie was looking at my intense inspection with one eyebrow raised. I put down the tart and cleared my throat. "I'm pretty sure we can get Carol off today after I give my declaration that I saw someone else at the scene. I'm an eyewitness that someone else was there at the time Jackson would have been murdered."

Ethel sniffed away the tears that threatened to fall out of her baby blue eyes. "Eye witness? Someone else? Of course we all know Carol couldn't have done this right?"

We all shook our heads in agreement.

"What did you see?" Ethel asked.

Although the curtains were tied tight and nothing hummed but the stove light, I felt the need to look over my shoulder before I spoke.

I leaned in closer and whispered. "Okay so when I was outside smoking cigarettes *that I don't officially smoke if you see my dad*... I saw this figure outside Jackson's house – only I didn't know it was Jackson's house at the time. I thought he might be throwing up from some bad chili because he was hunched over, but then I realize he was hunched over because he was sneaking around! When I caught his eye- he *came running at me*. At the time I didn't understand why this guy might want to hurt me, but now I know it's probably because I saw him and could put him at the scene of the crime."

Ethel and Dodie leaned in absorbed by my story. I realized in all the murder chaos and chili cook-off blue medal winning, I had forgotten to tell them about any of this.

I reported everything that had happened with the strange man and the knife – especially my skillful bottle cap slinging. "Anyway he was all dressed in black and had a ski mask on so that's all I know."

When I finished Dodie looked at Ethel and placed her hand over mine. "You poor thing you must have been terrified!"

"What did he look like?" Ethel remained focused.

"Well, he was all dressed in black," I said, "and he had a ski mask on, so that's all I know."

Dodie and Ethel looked at each other and shook their heads.

"How come you didn't say anything at the chili cook-off about that?" said Ethel.

"Well it happened so fast, and I was in shock, and…well, and then the arrest…"

"So you think the man with the knife might be the real culprit?" said Ethel.

I nodded. "I'm supposed to give a statement to that Six

Pines police officer today, Det. Fuzzbottom."

I made a face.

Dodie asked, "Do you know him?"

"I had a run-in with him before, and he was the officer at the scene that arrested Carol. He wants to question me."

Ethel nodded. "He'll want you to identify the other suspect and the time you saw him at the house."

Dodie thought about it. "Are you a suspect too?"

"Me?" Good grief I hadn't even considered that. "I hope not!" I blurted.

Dodie took my hand. "No, don't worry about it. You were with us at the chili cook-off the whole time, and then you were with Jaime. Everybody saw you."

I sighed. "Right."

"Besides, it seems as if you may have seen the real murderer. Thank God you weren't hurt Kat! Just go in and tell the police exactly what you told us. Remember you were almost a victim too."

My eyes widened at the thought. It was true.

Who knows what might have befallen me if I hadn't been a pro beer bottle snapper?

These were strange occurrences that had never tainted even the outskirts of Kissing Bridge before. Poor Mr. Jennings dead, sweet Carol blamed, and a bloody crockpot that no one would ever want to touch again.

Ethel was distraught. "Well, we need to get her free and I hope your information is the key, Kat. They wouldn't even grant her bail yesterday; poor Carol is sitting in a cell right now." Ethel's big blue eyes swelled up again with tears.

I felt her pain. Carol was one in a billion. She was kind and generous and smart and she always had your back. Carol had never had children of her own, so if she liked you, she took you under her wing like a real fairy grandmother and you got to call her *Aunty.*

When my mom passed away fifteen years ago, Carol urged me into the choir with her. She took me to her scrapbooking circle at Maxine's shop to keep me busy. Dad worked a lot, and I found solace scrapbooking old memories of our family in better times, trying to piece together the loss. I spent many tear-filled nights being comforted by Carol and pasting away my pain. Carol and Maxine had been friends of my mothers, and now officially, they were friends of mine too.

I truly adored "Aunty" Carol for so many reasons. I knew in my heart that she couldn't have killed anyone, and I was going to make it my mission to get her out of jail, but we had to find the real murderer first.

And I knew just where to start; because we had an ace in our hand the murderer hadn't counted on.

CHAPTER 19

E thel Landers.

She was our ace in the hole, and our answer to finding the real killer of Jackson Jennings.

It was well known that the Landers women got together every Sunday for brunch, and watched their favorite movie - *Breakfast at Tiffany's*.

You'd think they'd get sick of it.

But it was true. Every Sunday. Morning.

Every Sunday morning they closed the bakery and they got together and watched *Breakfast at Tiffany's* while they taste tested out new recipes together and had family time. The movie was so ingrained in their psyches they could mouth the words to the entire movie while they watched it - like their own version of the Rocky Horror Picture Show, only much more elegant and with delicious tasting real treats. Some of their best recipes came out of those *Sunday Breakfast at Tiffany's brunches*.

But a little know tradition of the Landers ladies, was that

of the marathon taking to the bed episodes. Only the real insiders, such as myself, knew about this tradition. My mother had been in attendance at one of the events and had kept me captivated by the stories of what went on at the Landers house between four bedposts and a good plasma screen TV.

When things got overwhelming in the outside world, Landers women sought the refuge of their bed.

The bed was like their own safety zone oasis, where they could hide away and create a buffer against difficult times. Whenever things got rough for the Landers ladies, they had a bad day, or plain old melancholy – the antidote was always the same – *take to the bed.*

The – *taking to the bed* routine consisted of staying in bed for a day – sometimes more - where the *bed-dee* was treated like British royalty taking refuge in their boudoir. The *bed-dee* was brought food to her bedside, and allowed to binge watch whatever she wanted on Netflix. Her attendees were usually the immediate family, but close friends were known to join in because some good food and rowdy times were had at bedside.

Each of the Landers ladies had their own favorite shows to help them feel better when they took to the bed. While Summer enjoyed old Baywatch reruns, and Aunt Carol liked the mean cooking guy show, Ethel was all about

Murder She Wrote marathons.

Ethel had actually watched every single episode of *Murder She Wrote ever made.* In fact she watched all 12 Seasons consisting of 264 episodes five times over before they took it off Netflix. Of course Summer bought her the box set for Christmas, so who knew how many times she was up to now.

The point I'm trying to make is: Ethel Landers Elkins was a certified *Murder She Wrote* expert.

Although it wasn't criminology class, right now, I'd take all the TV crime school help I could get. I was counting on her to help answer the many questions we still had about Jackson's murder, and finding the real killer so we could free Aunt Carol.

I looked at Ethel expectedly. "Ethel, I think we need to count on ourselves to find the real murderer. I don't trust that stupid Fuzzbottom. He seemed too quick to accuse Aunt Carol."

Dodie took a sip of coffee. "Well she was holding the crockpot that killed him."

We both looked at her. This kind of talk wasn't helping.

"Ethel," I continued, "you're the expert on murders, what would that old lady do...?"

Ethel knit her brow together, that appeared to be her *go to look* whenever she was kind of upset, and didn't know what was going on. She seemed bewildered that we were turning to her for advice. "Whatever do you mean?"

Dodie spoke up. "She's talking about your innate detective skills Ethel! You're the resident expert on amateur sleuthing via your *Murder She Wrote* marathons! You can always answer all the questions every time we get one on trivia!"

The magnitude of the bed episodes and her *Murder She Wrote marathons* was beginning to dawn on Ethel.

She smirked, and looked at us both with a new interest. She straightened her dress and sat up taller, exalted by her newfound importance. "Well I never thought about it like that, but I suppose I do know some things about solving a murder – but it is TV."

"Look -," I said, "you're as close to an expert we have on this! Jaime's got his hands tied 'cause it's out of his jurisdiction. So think. What would that old lady do *if it were her sister accused of croaking somebody with a crockpot?*"

CHAPTER 20

E thel thought about it.

The silence stretched out for what seemed like an eternity. Finally she cleared her throat and looked at us both with a new determination.

"First of all," Ethel took a sip of her tea, "her name is Jessica - let's be respectful here. She's a fabulous actress and she was tremendous in the part. So what would Jessica do? Well..."

The thinking resumed. This time it seemed it'd take a week. I suddenly wanted a cigarette I wasn't supposed to have. Instead I got up and made another pot of coffee and put it in the warm carafe. I steamed up some heavy cream to bring on the side, and added a liberal dash of Irish Bailey's liquor. It seemed to be exactly what we needed right now. But you know how I feel about liquor and food and beverage.

Again, that's my personal secret. It's not like I'm going to reveal my hard learned lessons to the Landers about my French liquor training. Not that we're competing against each other, but let's just say I'd like to earn some credit here in Kissing Bridge as a real chef.

I thought about that night at the Six Pines Chili Cook-Off. Ethel looked at me seriously now, feeling promoted in her the knowledge that she actually had some clout and ability in the detective department.

"Okay - let's start with the figure you saw by the house, Kat."

I nodded.

"Because they're obviously going to ask you about the figure you saw crouching by Jackson's house, and that's the most important thing to get Carol off. You're an eyewitness that can put somebody else at the scene. Right there we've established reasonable doubt."

Sounded good. I took another bite of my tart. "So I just tell Fuzzbottom the truth about how I saw some guy crouched down looking like he was puking," I said, "but then he must have been fine because he came after me. So he needs to find that guy."

Dodie listened from her position at the stove, as she pulled out a saucepan and cracked some eggs into it expertly. I watched her grinding up some fresh tarragon to put in the scrambled eggs, and the smell of the herbs lifted my senses with its fresh bite. I watched her as she rubbed a fresh piece of garlic out of its skin like a lover, and then diced it apart. Like my love life.

Girls can't live on sweets alone and these were stressful times. It looked like we were having a two-course breakfast sleuthing session. Eating always seemed to help, and a good crisis is the perfect time for complete calorie denial.

"Kat do you remember what time it was that you saw the person outside of Jackson's house?" asked Ethel. "The Detective is sure to ask you that, and it's going to be important to absolve Carol."

 I thought about it. "Well, we hadn't won the semifinals yet, and we were out of chili, so I went out to have a cigarette." I glared at both of them. "*Again* don't tell my dad about that... so maybe 6:45? I think we should take notes..."

I pulled out my phone, but Ethel and Dodie's heads both shot up.

"No!" they cried in unison. I looked back and forth between them, and put my cell phone away.

Ethel continued. "First of all I think better when I'm using my hands and writing something down. Old fashioned I know, but it's worked for hundreds of years and that's what I'm going to use."

Dodie nodded emphatically in agreement, as she scooped the scrambled eggs onto three plates, and sprinkled some fresh crumbled Greek feta and bright orange carnelian edible flowers on top. "No cell writing for sure, there's that whatever *electronic trail thing* to consider," she added.

I shrugged my shoulders. Okay, whatever. I had no idea about electronic trails but they won't let that Snowden guy back in the country after he said everyone was spying on us. For all I knew the toaster was taking down everything we said right now.

"Good old pen and paper sound good to me," I said.

I stood up and walked over and grabbed one of the waitress' checkbooks and a pen from the back counter, looking at the toaster in a whole new light.

I sat back down and got down to business. I wrote:

"#1 Way to Get Carol Free: Find the other suspect at the scene. Got it."

I looked at Ethel and a thought occurred to me.

"When Fuzzbottom was arresting Carol she told me that she went to Jackson's house because he sent her a note."

Ethel nodded. "Yes some man in the crowd handed Summer a note with Carol's name on it and Jackson's family seal. Summer told me."

She looked at Dodie and me and continued. "Jackson always uses a red wax to seal his important letters. That way people can't just lick it and reseal. Who has a problem with that I wouldn't know but that was his reasoning. Anyway Summer gave it to Carol right before she ran out the door for the backup crockpots from the van."

"Bingo!" I said. "Last night when they were arresting her – Aunt Carol said that the note said something about it being a – *life and death situation*– and he had her crockpot hostage!"

Ethel's blue eye's illuminated with an idea. "That letter is all we need to show she was put at the scene not that she proactively went after Jackson! So where is the letter? Did she tell you Kat?"

I shook my head. I wondered why Carol hadn't produced the letter herself to avoid arrest.

We all looked at each other. Where was the letter? That was a good question. Dodie served us the breakfast and sat down with us to figure out the puzzle. I refilled our coffee cups from the carafe.

Ethel folded her napkin on her lap like a true lady; I just dug in and started shoveling, because I'm not. I took another bite of Dodie's eggs and swooned. Good grief these women could cook like a dream!

Dodie took a bite of her scrambled eggs and nodded in approval at the taste. A thought hit her and she looked up at us. "But, wasn't the letter on Carol's person somewhere? Shouldn't the detective have found that letter and put it in evidence?"

Ethel took a sip of her tea and considered it. "Yes – if they found it. The only evidence they seem to have is the crockpot – which isn't good."

Dodie thought about it.

"Maybe it fell out of her pocket. You were there Kat – did you see any letter on the ground?"

I flashed back on the scene and nibbled on the fresh scone Dodie had baked to accompany the eggs.

"...There were lots of pots and pans, and stuff on the floor like someone had been looking for something, but I didn't notice any piece of paper in that mix...then again, the guy croaked by the crockpot was kind of taking up all my attention. So who knows? Poor old man."

I shook my head at the memory. I couldn't dispel the thought of those bright red carrots in his shock white hair. I made a note never to put carrots in my chili again.

Ethel pondered our next move. "In this situation in the show, Jessica always goes back and searches the crime scene. The police CSI team should've been doing that last night."

"So then they might've found the letter?" I asked hopefully.

We all looked at each other. Carol was still in jail. If the letter had been discovered, surely she would've made bail.

Ethel continued. "I think we need to go back to Jackson's house, and find that note – then we have some real proof that could surely clear Carol's name!"

I wasn't really relishing going back in that creepy house – for all I knew the corpse was still in there. But, Ethel was on a roll and had the detective background.

She turned to me and asked. "What time do you have to go down to Six Pines to talk to the detective?"

I took another bite of the heavenly breakfast Dodie had just *whipped up* easy peasy. It was delicious and I didn't taste one bit of liquor in it. Oh she was good.

I pointed to my plate enthusiastically. "Really please tell me we can put this on the new menu for the Enchanted Cozy Café – it's awesome!"

Ethel turned her nose down at me. "Stay focused Kat. What time is your appointment today?"

Dodie winked at me.

I swallowed. "He said to come in around two o'clock."

Ethel smiled. "Since you can't drive yourself, I think I should take you."

"If you want to drive me there that would be great."

Dodie put her fork down. "Wait, isn't the police station on the same block as the Pavilion Center...?"

My eyes lit up. "... *And* the same block as Jackson Jennings' house..."

Ethel's eyes were gleaming now.

"We're going to go early, and we're going to get into Jackson's house somehow, and see if we can find that letter and free Carol!"

As little as I wanted to engage in breaking and entering a murder scene – I knew the answer to freeing Carol might be in that house. I had to agree with Ethel. We needed to get back into Jackson's house and find out who wanted him killed, and find that letter to prove Carol's innocence.

I also wasn't really looking forward to running into Fuzzbottom again.

At least now I would have a sweet senior with me as social camouflage so maybe he'd be nicer.

Maybe.

CHAPTER 21

Ethel rolled up in front of my house at around noon and beeped the bakery van horn three times to signal to me that it was her. *As if* I'd made plans with someone else.

It was a clear day in Kissing Bridge, and the temperature wasn't freezing so I didn't need a scarf. I decided to let Aphrodite come with me anyway because she loved to drive in the car, and because I thought I might appear more sympathetic to Fuzzbottom.

Some guys have a weakness for cute kittens; I've seen it happen before. Aphrodite always drew admiration for her beauty. Maybe her baby blues could woo Fuzzbottom if mine couldn't.

Soon we are on way down the hill in the bakery van, and headed towards Six Pines Valley.

We were both kind of excited about our first breaking and entering – with good cause mind you – and we were warming up to the idea of being amateur sleuths.

We had debated the best way to sneak in to Jackson's house. I suggested to Ethel that she could act like a crazy old forgetful woman who thought it was her house and she had misplaced her keys – "Oh, the woes of losing one's memory" – and all that. Ethel just wanted me to sing really loudly while she broke a window with Earl's grandson's baseball bat.

In the end we didn't need to use either of our awesome ideas. Dr. Branson Archibald, Carol's husband, had stopped by the bakery later that morning to bring Ethel up to speed on the investigation. He confirmed that no note had been found, and yes it was important. Seems Carol still had the key to Jackson's house on her keyring – clearly marked – in her dresser drawer. Not good for the Six Pines investigators to know, but it sure made it easier for us to get in.

CHAPTER 22

We parked a couple blocks away from the main street where Jackson's house and the police station were. Jackson's land actually spanned miles, but the house was smack in the middle of the populated downtown Six Pines.

We had both worn drab clothes so as not to pull any unneeded attention to ourselves. Other than the white cat I was wearing around my neck and the baseball bat Ethel insisted she use as an *old lady cane prop/possible weapon,* we looked perfectly normal.

The main street in Six Pines was called Six Pines Alley. As you can imagine, it was lined with rows of towering pines that seemed to protect the little historic cobbled street packed with quaint shops and some wealthy homes. The pines' green needles were vibrant against the backdrop of the white-capped Kissing Bridge Mountains. Too bad the trees hadn't done much good protecting old Mr. Jennings.

****

That said, they were great cover for us.

Ethel and I snuck in through the back forest and unlocked the old door quietly. The house was creepily quiet and had the feeling of emptiness. Despite the fact that Jackson had money, his house was sparsely furnished in an old fashioned colonial style – really, who has that kind of taste? It looked like his mother and father had bought it and he never replaced it after their deaths. Maybe he was sentimental. Most likely he was cheap like everybody said.

Only dim light bled through drawn curtains and an air of dust and death stifled me. I put my hand over my mouth because I thought I might barf. Ethel seemed fine with the possibility of turning the corner and seeing Jackson's dead body still lying there, but I felt queasy.

We made our way slowly into the kitchen, dreading the scene before us.

Luckily, Jackson's dead body was no longer there, but the chili and disheveled contents of the cabinets and kitchen items still littered the ground. Now stark yellow tape marked off the area where Jackson's body had lain like in an episode of CSI.

There's a really creepy feeling when you're in a place that somebody was murdered in. I know I had been there when he was *just killed,* but there had been so much activity, it was hard to feel anything at the time but shock. Now walking into the scene of the crime again, the enormity of what had happened and the finality of it made me choke up.

Who had done this to this poor old man?

Ethel whispered for us to branch out and cover the paths Carol might have taken on the way in. I was going to go out through the front door and come up the path. From there I would climb the rickety front porch stairs and try and retrace Carol's steps. Ethel was starting with the kitchen and working backwards, prepared to scour every inch of the path that Carol had traversed.

The note could have fallen out anywhere in the house. For that matter, it could've fallen out on the street! I went out the front door and peeled my eyes to the pavement, looking for anything that might resemble a letter on the ground. Next, I looked back and forth as I made my way up the old porch stairs. They were wooden with spaces between them where you could see the dark ground beneath the deck. I peered into the darkness between the cracks but I couldn't spot a thing. I continued up the stairs, sneaking a look down the cobbled street, which luckily was deserted. The steps used to be gray, but they had been painted over with a deep green. You could still see the old color through the worn off spots of green. It looked like nobody loved this house. I hadn't even known that Jackson had a residence in Six Pines. He had been staying up at Eagle's Peak Lodge as long as anyone could remember.

I next perused the stale-smelling living room, but to no avail. It wasn't long before I was right back where I started, in the kitchen and face-to-face with Ethel. She looked at me with a hopeful look. I shook my head.

Where could it be, where could it be?

And what would Jessica do in this situation?

I felt the need to whisper for some reason. "If we can't find the note itself, maybe we can find the person who handed Summer the note in the first place? That might be enough to clear her. Did Summer say what the person looked like who handed her the note?"

Ethel shook her head and leaned on her cane/bat.

"She doesn't remember much. She was so busy signing autographs she can't remember the face."

A loud thud pounded from the old ceiling above us. We flinched. Somebody was upstairs. I grabbed onto Ethel. "What was that?"

She put her finger to her mouth and motioned for me to hide behind the curtains with her. Within moments, Helena, Jackson's sister, and her son Frankie thundered down the second floor stairs. I recognized them from the night they came storming into the café with Jackson.

"What are you two doing here?!" Frankie barked.

I glanced at Ethel from behind the curtain and shrugged. We both looked down to see our feet sticking out of the bottom of the red velvet draperies. Aphrodite chose that moment to be a total traitor and let out a loud MEEOW. I'm pretty sure Jessica Fletcher never hid so ineptly.

I pulled the curtains back. The gig was up. We looked at them, and they looked at us.

"What are you doing here, Helena?" Ethel said irritated.

Helena was indignant. "I grew up in this house! I was looking for something that's mine that I can't find and it's...it's none of your business! What are *you* doing here?!"

Before we could answer, yet another voice alarmed us – this one deep and male. "People! What are you all doing here? This is a crime scene!"

We all looked at each other.

Jaime Henderson was standing at the door in his uniform. He stared at us incredulously and then took a slow step inside. "I was just stopping by the Six Pines station to give my story and I thought I passed the bakery van parked a few blocks back. I was hoping I was wrong." He scowled at us and shook his head. "Kat –

Ethel, you can't just go breaking into a crime scene!"

Jaime eyed Ethel's cane/bat suspiciously. I figured that was our cue to go. I grabbed Ethel's arm as if I was aiding her and she shook me off and gave me *the look*. I guess she was done acting helpless.

"You're not helping Carol's case by breaking and entering," said Jamie.

Ethel murmured under her breath, "We had the key."

I elbowed her to keep her mouth shut. Jaime wasn't turning us in, but if we got caught here by Fuzzbottom it might be another story.

"Come on. You too folks." Jaime waved for Helena and Frankie to follow us out.

"This is my family home and I still have personal items here that I would like to retrieve." Helena crossed her arms.

Jaime guided us out the door. "Family or not, this is still an active investigation, and I'm sure they'll grant you access after they're done."

We all filed out reluctantly. Jaime locked the door to Jackson's house behind him, and we were all left standing outside looking at each other. What a failure. We hadn't found the letter, and I had to go talk to Fuzzbottom.

CHAPTER 23

Soon I was face-to-face across from Fuzzbottom, and actually he was even more unattractive the third time around. The lights in the Six Pines' police station are not flattering. I don't know if their fluorescent or some special horrible looking bulbs that are purposely meant to make you look extra bad. Maybe they were supposed to make you look like a con?

I could only imagine what I looked like if Fuzzbottom looked this bad. The harsh lighting above the office desk made his skin appear a weird ashen color, and the bags under his eyes were so deep it looked like he had been on a drinking binge. His cheeks were flushed too red, with breaking capillaries which bespoke an Irish heritage. I had seen that look before on heavy drinkers. Thank goodness I knew enough not to drink until my face turned red and chunky because I'm vain.

Obviously Fuzzbottom had given up on his looks a while ago, although he didn't look much older than twenty-five. I noticed that his neck looked extra hairy now that I was sitting across from him. I could see that his thick dark arm hair actually stuck out from the bottom of his shirt cuffs, a good two inches long and onto his hands.

Yuck.

I wanted to gag. I couldn't imagine being his poor girlfriend and being fondled with those hairy hands.

He eyed Aphrodite wrapped around my neck, purring, but he looked away from her beguiling gaze and got down to business.

"Let's start from the beginning."

I squirmed in the uncomfortable chair. "Okay, so we were all at the big chili cook-off when Carol went to get her backup crockpot out of the van, but it went missing and she never came back. I'm sure that's the reason why she went over to Jackson's house."

Det. Fuzzbottom studied me closely, and his muddy eyes seemed to distrust me.

"So you knew Carol was going over there to kill Jackson." He stated it as a fact.

"Wha–no! I said I knew Carol must be somewhere, and the only thing I knew was that Jackson had sent her some ominous note about kidnapping her crockpot and a matter of life or death...."

He stopped me. "What note?"

"Jackson has a special red insignia seal that he puts on all his letters. Someone gave a note from him to Summer to give to Carol. But didn't you find the note in your investigation? Carol told her husband she had it in her pocket. Did you check her coat?"

Fuzzbottom's rat-like brown eyes glared at me."You accusing me of not doing my job?"

I gulped, and a little squeak came out of Aphrodite.

"No, sir!" I said. "I mean, that note is super important, and it *has to be somewhere*. Lots of people knew it existed, and it proves…"

Fuzzbottom held up a hand making a hairy stop sign in my face.

"I think that you better spend your time getting your own alibi together, Ms. Katherine O'Hara, and less time butting your big head in where it doesn't belong."

Ouch. That *big head* thing was a sore spot with me.

I'd been teased about that since I was a kid. *Ogre head O'Hara.* Thus the bangs I'd worn since I was old enough to grow hair. *Whatever,* dude looked like he could be the *missing link!* I wasn't going to take his insults personally. I absent-mindedly pushed my bangs down over my forehead hoping to hide as much face as possible.

Fuzzbottom looked like he wanted to swat me.

"I think I may have seen the real murderer," I blurted out.

Fuzzbottom sighed, but waved at me to continue.

"Last night I was outside having a cigarette..."

At Fuzzbottom's glazed look I hurried on.

"Well there was this man – in black, and he wasn't too happy I saw him. He came after me with a knife and he should have a mark from my bottle cap that will prove..."

I continued through the whole story of my assailant and my epic bottle-cap-slinging defense. I finally seemed to catch his interest when I mentioned the man I had seen crouching by the house the same time Jackson's murder occurred. I thought Jaime had reported it to the Six Pines police, but it seemed like news to Fuzzbottom.

He stopped writing on his pad and put down his pen. He leaned over the desk and looked me in the eye. "So now you're saying there was a masked knife-wielding ninja that leapt at you – who you disabled with an improvised lethal weapon?"

"Well, I wouldn't call a bottle cap a lethal weapon, officer, that's a little harsh..."

I was shaking so much at this turn around I prayed he didn't hear the cache of bottle caps I kept in my coat pocket rattling around. I eyed Aphrodite and she shook her head.

"Besides, Det. Fuzzbottom, I think you're focusing on the wrong thing here. That man is the possible murderer of Jackson, and I was the victim."

"Do you have any wounds to prove your victim-ness?"

My eyebrow rose. Victim-ness? Proof? "Well, no..."

"How about eye witnesses to corroborate your self-defense story?"

"No." I said defeatedly.

"Well let's just hope then, for your sake, *Big Head,* that no one comes forward wanting to press charges against you for attacking them when it seems the poor person was just excitedly trying to get some chili through the front door!"

"Oh, come on!" I groaned.

He slammed his police notebook shut with force enough to cause a little wind to lift my bangs. I self-consciously patted them back down again. He looked up at me.

"I don't think you're taking this murder seriously," he went on. "I don't give a rat's butt about the chili cook-off or your own personal issues with our wonderful Six Pines' neighbors. We have a dead man's body that was knocked out and beaten with a crockpot that was in the hands of your boss. If and when you can bring me anything that is actual *evidence* to the contrary, then please do. Until then, for all our sakes – just stay in Kissing Bridge where you belong. We don't like out-of-towners abusing our locals with their concealed weapons. Now leave before I decide to book you based on your own confession."

Aphrodite sunk her claws into me and I rose in haste.

Oh boy, oh boy, did I want to throw out some of my practiced French rudeness on Fuzzbottom right now. I really think I could have gotten away with it too because I know a couple *really rude French words* that I'm pretty sure he wouldn't understand, but I wasn't taking any chances in his case.

I held my tongue and hurried to get out of his office bent on a quick get away.

CHAPTER 24

I threw open the door of Fuzzbottom's office, and Ethel almost fell on the floor. She recovered nicely, belying her earlier gymnastic years, and straightened up like a pro.

"Ethel!" I exclaimed. "Goodness – what are you..." I thought she had been waiting for me in the car where it was warm and toasty.

She looked at me with chagrin. She'd been spying. I suddenly had a new respect for this snappy senior.

Fuzzbottom wasn't happy.

"What were you doing out there?" he queried the innocent looking elder. "How did you get in here?"

He looked down the hall as if he were going to yell at someone, caught sight of his Captain, fake smiled, and then glared at us.

He looked at me and hissed, "Who is she?"

I tried to figure out the best lie to least implicate Ethel. After all, her sister was a suspected murderer being held some-where in this very building. Maybe it ran in the family.

Ethel answered for herself. "Well hello, Detective. I was just telling my old friend from high school – your Captain Sykes, that this interview was going awfully long, and I really need to get home to get my medicine."

My brow shot up. I'm pretty sure that was a lie. The only medicine I ever saw Ethel take was in the form of a scone or extra cookie with her chamomile tea. I tried to reposition my face so I looked normal.

Fuzzbottom was looking back and forth at us both now like he thought something was wrong but couldn't quite put his finger on it. The mention of Ethel knowing his Captain had taken away his egotistical bravado, and he just waved us away with a, "Don't be leaving town I'm going to want to talk to you again."

We shuffled out of the door hurriedly.

Ethel stopped at the front desk as we passed and blew a kiss to the Captain. "Come in for breakfast when we open, Harry, and bring your wife with you. I'd love to see her again."

"Will do, Ethel! Tell Earl I'll see him next week at the convention!"

"Oh, and Harry," she continued, "if you come across that letter we talked about or have more news on that lurking individual, please call me."

Harry tipped his hat. She smiled sweetly and I looked back over my shoulder to catch Fuzzbottom hanging out of his little office, taking in the interaction with his mouth curled in a snarl.

CHAPTER 25

It was raining again in Six Pines, and it drenched us as we ran to the van.

Ethel jacked the car into drive and rolled up the mountain. The road home was windy and tree-lined and felt solitary and lonely. I think we were both thinking about Carol and that cell. Kissing Bridge just had a Mayberry RFT one-room kind of deal because there is no real crime that gets committed there. But Six Pines was a bigger city, so we had no idea what a cell there might look like. Poor Carol.

Ethel shook her head. "I was so happy when I recognized Harry, but there wasn't much he could do. They don't have that letter, and that's her only alibi."

"And we have no idea who that guy lurking around was that came after me was either."

"So right now there is no other suspect than Carol," Ethel confirmed.

"Hey!" A bright idea hit me. "That guy that gave Summer the letter from Jackson – she said all she remembered was that he was wearing a white shirt and black pants."

Ethel waited.

"That's standard uniform for most upscale restaurants... maybe he works for one of the restaurants here that entered the contest!"

Ethel's face brightened. "We could get a list of the contestants from the city council. They run the contest and donate the money to local charities."

I pulled out our black-and-white tiger-striped notebook that was our designated planner. I wrote down – *Get list of contestants.*

Another thought occurred to me. "I could go down the list and call each of them and ask them what their dress code was at the contest."

Ethel nodded. "Great idea. Chances are the killer was at the contest spying on Jackson and then followed him home."

I thought about it.

Flakes of snow began to fall on the van window and I knew we were nearing the peaks of Kissing Bridge. The pines grew more majestic here and their emerald beauty stretched out on either side of the road. I just couldn't get that figure chasing me out of my mind. Somewhere, someone was walking around with a souvenir from my bottle cap bullet.

"Let's go back to the guy I saw. He was over at Jackson's the same time Carol was there. I know because I was using looking for Carol as an excuse to catch a quick cigarette."

Ethel shot me a glare. "In the middle of the contest, how could you?"

"I was rattled – and Aunt Carol was missing – and if I hadn't then I wouldn't have seen the other person sneaking around Jacksons!"

Ethel had to concede to that point, so she let it go. "Did you talk to Jaime about the possible other suspect?"

I nodded. "Yeah, 'cause the guy chased me and I was freaked out, that's why we went together to look for Carol. The problem is this isn't his jurisdiction. This is Six Pines, so they have their own team."

"Are you sure it was a man?"

"Pretty sure, he was much bigger than me...darn, Ethel, it was dark and I don't wear glasses 'cause I'm vain. I think it was a man... the main concern should be that there IS another suspect. I can put him at the scene at the same time as the murder, so shouldn't that get Carol out?"

Ethel considered.

"Not until they actually have him I wouldn't think. You saw someone and they came after you, but my sister was the one over his dead body with the crockpot."

CHAPTER 26

We drove a long way without saying much. My phone rang. I looked down to see Elle's name.

Elle was my bestie, and she ran the Eagle's Peak lodge along with her grandfather Earl, Ethel's new husband.

I had gotten to thinking after the murder that it was odd that Jackson's sister, Helena, grew up here, but had never bothered to visit, except the day before her brother died. I had wondered if we needed to consider her as a suspect? She didn't seem to like her brother so why was she here? Maybe she was after his money? She looked well off, and the family was known to have money. But Jackson was oil rich; they'd found it on his acreage right there in Six Pines. That was a *whole other kind of rich*.

I wondered if she could have had someone kill her brother for the money? Did she hate him that much? And what about her son? He was big enough to have been the man I saw. Where was he during the murder, and did he have a telling bottle cap wound somewhere on his body as a reminder?

I had called Elle, and asked her to check and see if any of the new lodgers up at the Eagle's Peak Lodge met the description of Jackson's sister and nephew. It made sense to me that anyone with money and any sense would stay up at the Eagle's Peak lodge. The lodge had the nicest rooms and was always full of excitement because it was at the bottom of the hill and right next to the ski shop.

I smiled when she told me the news. "Bingo!" I cheered as I waved frantically at Ethel to take the turn onto Eagle's Peak Lane that led to the mountaintop and the lodge. She swerved left and headed up.

"Thanks, Elle." I hung up and beamed over at Ethel. "Jackson's sister and her son are staying at the lodge. Elle said she just sat them down for a late lunch – and that Mia girl too."

"Who's Mia?"

"She's Jackson's fiancée, *the Poodle*. I told you about her. She's the one that was with him at the café the other night when he came in and was hissing a fit over finding Carol. Remember I came in the next morning – you and Carol were making strawberry crème puffs?"

Sometimes it was better to talk to Ethel in food terms. Everything seemed to crystalize around food and color.

She perked up. "Yes, yes, the icing I made was the most precious pink – we'll have to make some for Summer's baby shower."

"Isn't Summer having a boy?"

Ethel waved it off. "He won't be eating it, all the ladies that come will be. And goodness knows ladies love pink."

I couldn't argue with her there.

"So what about this Mia?" she said.

"Well, Jackson was parading her around with a big ring on her finger but she didn't look very happy. Had that goth chick look. Pale skin, dark hair, wore all black. I think she had a nose piercing?"

Ethel scrunched her nose at the thought of it. Suddenly her eyes lit up. "The girl from the chapel!"

I had no idea what she was talking about. I scrambled to understand. "The chapel..."

"When we got married, a girl stood up after Carol stopped the wedding and said she was Jackson's girlfriend – and that she was pregnant!"

"Pregnant?"

Wow, I sat back in the bucket seat. I didn't see that coming.

CHAPTER 27

Ethel turned the corner and headed up the last pass to the lodge. The epic peaks were in full view.

"Why would a young thing like that want to marry and have old man Jennings's baby?"

We looked at each other. There was only *one reason* and it wasn't his scintillating personality.

"If she has his child, that's going to be his only heir," I said.

Ethel said it first. "Then she is on the top of the list of suspects. Murders always have a motive, and nothing motivates like money."

I nodded. Ethel would know. She was the *Murder She Wrote* officiando.

"But maybe she's not the only one that could benefit from Jackson's money," I added. "There was definitely no love lost between Jackson and his sister either. She really hates him – I think we need to consider her."

Ethel's eyes narrowed. "How do you know?"

I shrugged. "Spidey sense I guess. She has real expressive lines on her face and they are like a roadmap of her feelings. And they all looked like they hated Jackson. I don't know if she's capable of murdering her own brother, but we need to find out why she came here and what exactly their relationship was."

"Agreed. So why would they be having lunch with Mia?"

"Good question," I said. "It doesn't sound like a family get together to mourn the loss of a loved one."

The lodge came into full view as we headed up the last of the mountain road.

The Eagle's Peak Lodge was over two hundred years old. It was made from solid oak trunks, and lots of love. The Elkins' family had owned and managed the lodge for generations. It was a popular hangout in Kissing Bridge, with the best ski lifts, bed and breakfast accommodations, and a wonderful diner that looked out over the base of the tallest ski mountain in Vermont.

Cars clogged the parking lot where we pulled in and

skiers were in various stages of ski clothes to go up the hill or ripped off wet layers to go home. The snow was coming down hard up on the mountain, and the lodge looked cherry with the light of the fire's glow inside.

Ethel parked the van, and I took Aphrodite off my neck and put her in her cat carrier. She was not happy about that, but I was having none of her sass. I had serious business to attend to, and I also knew the inside of her carrier looked like something out of *I Dream of Genie's* bottle. It was lux to the max and had her favorite food to keep her mollified. I was proud of myself. I was getting good at being a cat lady – which also horrified me. Had I given up on love then?

Ethel waved to her husband Earl as he came through the big wooden doors of the Eagle's Peak Lodge to meet us. Elle must have let him know we were coming.

I grabbed Ethel's hand to get her attention. "Okay we're going to go in there and find out what's going on."

"Great. How do you suggest we do that?"

"Elle saved us a table right next to their booth. We're going to sit down and just be friendly – just like we are in Kissing Bridge. And you be a nosey old lady."

Ethel nodded." I can do that."

"We need to find out more about why they really came

to Kissing Bridge, and whether or not Mia is really pregnant." I said. "Just be as rude as you need to be, old ladies can get away with that." Ethel raised her eyebrow and it reminded me of my mother when she thought I was being classless.

"If only Carol's eavesdropping talent were here," she whispered.

I opened the car door.

Earl Elkins walked across the parking lot in long strides to meet us. He looked like a real authentic cowboy. He had a solid jaw and stood a good six foot four. Even for his age he was strong and sure and he made a perfect couple with his new wife Ethel.

I had warned Ethel to keep our little plan private. Upsetting her new husband wasn't going to help anything. Ethel took a deep breath and pulled out some perfume and sprayed a bit on her pulse. Earl sauntered over and opened the car door for her. She stepped out and he wrapped her in a big bear hug embrace. "Nice to see you, sweetheart." His voice was compassionate. "How are you doing?"

Ethel hugged him back. What could she say? Her sister was accused of murder, things were looking bleak, and we were about to have lunch with someone that might be a killer.

CHAPTER 28

L uckily, Ethel didn't share that last part with Earl.

I waited for her up at the front desk and talked to my dear friend Elle. It was nice to see Elle. I hadn't had much time to spend with her since I'd gotten back. We promised to get together soon. When Ethel joined me, Elle made a show of greeting us professionally, and then led us through the dining room and winked at me as she sat us at the table *right next* to our group of suspects.

The suspects, Mia, Helena, and Frankie, were seated in a coveted booth. The booths were half circles and made of soft red leather with a view of the mountain through the windows that belonged in a dream.

We pretended to look at our menus, all the while casting furtive glances to the group next to us. Mia (The Poodle) was on the furthest side of the booth and she had her coat on still. I couldn't tell if she had a baby bump. Darn it, who wears a coat in a dining room? Maybe someone with something to hide?

Maybe she was just cold all the time because she was so

darn pale and skinny. I was happy to see a big cheeseburger in front of her because she looked like she needed it. But she didn't seem to really be eating; she just picked at a fry and stared ahead, ignoring the other two.

Jackson's sister was in black again, with pearls again, only now with a fox stole slung across her shoulders. *Humph.* Don't get all-uppity, lady, I have a fur stole as well and she's my best friend – *beat that.*

Her son was gobbling up his food and bedecked in even more Harvard wear. Did he go to college there or just get it from some internet store?

Nobody was saying anything at the table, and I was getting bored so I leaned over and broke the ice. I looked at Mia who was staring off into nowhere.

"Hey there, I like your nose ring," I said.

She leveled her eyes at me and focused, realized I was talking to her. I was all smiles. "It goes real nice with that black rose tattoo." Her hand flew to cover the tattoo on her shoulder. "Get that here in Kissing Bridge or did you have to go off the mountain for that?"

She mumbled, "Burning Man. A couple years ago."

I nodded emphatically like I just loved tattoos and nose ring combos. "Been meaning to go to Burning Man."

Whatever that was. Hippy festival I think. Fit her.

"Anyway, I met you the other night I think," I said.

She tried to place me...

"At the Enchanted Café before it opened..." I prompted.

She nodded and her eyes widened a bit, probably remembering me threatening them with the spatula.

'I'm Kat and this is my boss – *Ethel*."

I left off "Landers" as I thought it might not work in our favor, but I wasn't fooling anyone.

The lady in the fur stole got up from the booth and came over and stuck her hand out to Ethel. "I'm Helena Jennings Allman – and you're Ethel Landers-Elkins I believe." Ethel nodded. Unsure of what was coming next.

"Well, we weren't formally introduced at the house the other day. Seemed we both had something we were looking for at my brother's. Maybe we can be of help to each other?"

Ethel looked at me. I shrugged.

Helena continued amiably, crossing her delicate hands in front of her. "Landers-Elkins...hmm...then it's your sister that is currently in jail for the murder of my brother, is that correct?"

I swallowed. Ethel opened her mouth but nothing came out. Helena continued. "Please come join us and let me buy you lunch. My brother was a horrible man and your sister did us all a favor."

Ethel raised her eyebrows, but I saw the opportunity and was taking it. I jumped out of my seat and grabbed my coat and purse. "Well, thank you so much – *Helena,* is it?" I pumped her hand. "I fear we got off to a bad start the other day."

I fake-helped Ethel to her feet and scooted her to the booth. Helena made the introductions as Mia rolled her eyes and focused on dipping a fry into the ketchup over and over again. The Harvard guy, Frankie, merely grunted in our direction and buried himself in his cell phone. I had the luck of sitting next to Mr. Personality, which actually was a perfect time to size him up. He had a lot to gain, as did his mother, with the death of Jackson.

Frankie Allman was a young, strong man, big enough to be the person in black that had chased me with the knife. I scoured my brain trying to place him at the chili contest. A flash of his face – wearing a Harvard hat and chatting with one of the other teams – came to mind. What team was that? I thought hard – red shirts.... *The Bulldangos!* The steak house restaurant in the suburb of Six Pines, Sleepy Oaks! But where was he when Jackson was getting murdered? I looked down at his broad arms.

He had the strength to do it. I took off my coat, and he moved his coat over to make room for me. I caught a flash of a needle sticking out of the inside pocket of his Varsity jacket – again emblazoned with Harvard.

Why would he have a needle? Was he a drug addict? Maybe he poisoned Jackson to weaken him and then bludgeoned him with the crockpot? I decided to pry – after all, we were invited.

"So – I'm guessing you're a big Harvard fan or are you in school there?" I asked Frankie. He tore his gaze away from the phone at the mention of Harvard.

"I just got accepted actually. I start in September if..." He was stopped by his mother's firm grip coming down on his hand. I watched the blood drain out of it as she squeezed. Frankie stopped talking.

"Now, Frankie, we're here to get to know each other, so let's not get sidetracked."

Frankie made a scowl and went back to staring at his cell phone.

Elle came by with a pitcher of sparkling water and cocked her head in amusement to see us all together. I beamed at her. This was going fabulously.

Helena offered to buy us all champagne but we declined. We needed to stay on our toes and drinking at lunch was not going to help.

Ethel spoke up. "I want to let you all know that my sister is not responsible for the death of Jackson. We're going to find the real murderer and put whoever did this senseless crime behind bars. "

Helena looked at her, confused. "So you're saying that your sister is innocent and there are other suspects?"

I cut in smoothly, worried Ethel might have given away too much.

"Carol is innocent so that means the real killer is still out there. As far as we know, there are no other suspects..." I elbowed Ethel to keep quiet and looked around the table to see if the "other suspects" comment hit home.

They were all gazing at me blankly. I went ahead and asked them straight.

"Do any of you have any idea who might want to see Jackson dead?"

I looked at Mia and she shook her head. Helena burst out laughing. I think she was getting tipsy.

"Oh, this is rich. My brother made a life's work out of ripping people off and casting them aside and you wonder which one of his countless victims did it? Good luck. You've got a long list to consider, sweetheart." She drank some more champagne and laughed at herself.

Ethel and I looked at each other.

Frankie put his phone away and looked at us suspiciously. Now that he was looking at me straight on I could see the resemblance to his mother and the Jennings side. Harvard Boy was light haired with matching slit-like blue eyes. He had the same short stature as Jackson and, from what I could see, the same bad attitude.

Frankie said, "Let's just talk about the memorial and we'll let the lawyers do what they do. It will all be settled tomorrow when Mr. Maritime reads the will."

He looked at Mia with disgust. "I don't know why you're insisting on making this hard for everyone," Frankie went on. "You shouldn't even be allowed to be in the office when they read my uncle's will. We're the only blood relatives Jackson has and you're just a piece of white trash trying to cash in on his money. You're the one that probably killed him."

Mia pushed up from the table and Helena said, *"Frankie!"* Ethel and I were both focused on Mia's torso. The coat parted and I tried not to be obvious because she was so upset, but I had to get a look under that darn coat.

"*You* were the ones that were just here to get Jackson's money!" said Mia. "He told me all about your pathetic calls asking for help."

Helena stood up now too. She was unbalanced from too much champagne so she put her hand on the table to steady herself. I noticed the empty bottle in an ice bucket by the side of the booth. Had she drained it all?

"I only asked for what was mine!" she hissed. "He didn't have the right to keep my gift from my mother along with swindling us out of house and home. You're nothing! You're a girl he put a ring on her finger so he could get her sister jealous of the inheritance! You were just a passing stop on his roadway of destruction. Another notch on his belt." Mia's mouth grew tighter and tighter.

"You're such a fool." Helena trailed off into laughter now. "If you think you're getting your hands on my family's legacy, you got another thing coming!"

Mia's hands were shaking as she searched in her purse, preparing to leave. Ethel dropped her teacup nervously and it rattled as it fell back to the saucer.

"You know what, Helena?" said Mia. "I can't wait to see your face tomorrow at the reading of the will."

Helena dismissed her with a wave, which seemed to

cause her to lose all her steam, and she collapsed back into her seat.

"Go. Go away with your empty threats, Mia. Your little engagement ring and promise to be wed means nothing anymore. Believe me, we intend to inherit what is rightly ours, and it will be over my dead body that you see a penny of my family's money."

Helena's pretense at niceties had obviously come to an end. She was full of contempt and it showed. But was it aimed at Mia – or her brother?

Helena leaned forward and had an eye show down with Mia. She lowered her voice, and hissed out in a threatening whisper, "My brother was a horrible man he strung you along, dear. You're – well - you're beneath his station, really. He never would have married you."

Mia gave her a look I hadn't seen before coming from the poodle girl. Her eyes were deeply lined with black liner so she appeared almost sinister even in the bright daylight. I wondered if I had misjudged what this girl was capable of.

"Oh, but you're wrong," Mia said in a scary tone.

She flung up her tiny white pale hand and there next to her large engagement ring was another gold ring all lined with diamonds. We all stared and took in the beauty and the meaning of this. I opened my mouth as I realized it was a matching *wedding ring.*

Helena gasped and Frankie looked up to see Mia waving the proof in his face.

"We got married two days before Jackson died and he changed the will. I will see you tomorrow at Mr. Maritime's office. And when he reads that will, you two – will get nothing."

With that, she swung around and her coat parted to reveal a baby bump.

Mia was definitely married, and she was definitely pregnant.

CHAPTER 29

I ran out after Mia and stopped her in the parking lot as she was wiping the new snowfall off her window with one of those mittens that has fake fur with the scraper attached. Christmas gift probably. You got one every year up in this area. So maybe she was local after all.

"Hey Mia!" she looked up, realized it was me, and went back to removing the snow as if I hadn't spoken. I wasn't missing my chance. She might have a key to this murder, and I had to get it out of her. I'm usually not a fake person, but I realized that I'm actually getting pretty good at it.

I donned a fake look of concern – okay mostly fake. She was pregnant after all and young and her old man fiancé had just died. Who knew if she really cared for him? Maybe she was all alone? I suddenly felt bad for her. I had to remind myself that though she was pregnant, and married to Jackson; she also had the most to gain from his death. For all I knew I could be confronting a killer.

"I'm sorry about that business back there," I said. "They should be nicer to you now that you're family."

She looked at me with her deep brown eyes that were overly lined in black like a goth superhero and pulled her glove off. She wiped at her eyes, creating two black smeared pools down her cheeks. She couldn't have been more than twenty-two.

She didn't reply. She put her key in the car door to leave, and I hurried closer to stall her.

"Congratulations on your marriage, too. I'm – I'm sorry about Jackson." She stopped at the sincerity in my voice. She turned and took a couple steps closer to me.

"You saw him? After it happened – they said you and Jaime were the ones that came in and found him?"

I looked in her eyes but I couldn't read her emotions. Was she sad he was dead, or relieved? I looked at the ground, overcome by the memory of the sight.

"Yes. It was – horrible. I'm so sorry."

I pushed myself to ask her, woman to woman. I looked up.

"Did you love him Mia? Like, real love?"

She looked at me, trying to read me, and remained silent. I stumbled on reaching for any way to connect with her. "I mean, he was awfully old, and you're a pretty girl – I bet you could get a lot of guys your own age."

She snorted. "You know what – you're a bad liar, Kat. Anyone ever tell you that? You stink at it. I know what I look like. I know you probably think I'm creepy with my crazy goth style. But I've had worse – you know what I mean?"

I shook my head. I had no idea what she meant and she had already caught me lying once. She pulled open her black purse and took out a black lighter and a black cigarette case with a black skeleton on it. She certainly took this goth thing seriously.

Mia took a couple cigarettes out and leaned against the car and offered me one. I looked around guiltily but I needed to keep talking to her so of course I had to take whatever opportunity came up – even a cigarette in plain daylight.

I thought to mention that if she was pregnant then she shouldn't be smoking, but three days after the death of her fiancée didn't seem the proper time to preach.

"Why don't we share one?" I said. "I'm trying to quit." She laughed a sweet sound that reminded me of how young she was. I hadn't ever seen her smile, and she almost looked sweet with her innocent gap-toothed grin.

"Good idea." She lit it and blew out a long line of smoke. Her muscles relaxed as she inhaled again.

I tried to act casual as I asked, "So what did you mean worse...what's worse?"

Mia handed me the cigarette like we were old pals.

"Guys, silly. Guys can be jerks. That old man was nice to me. Jackson treated me like a real lady. I'm not used to that."

I kind of believed her. He'd been nice to Carol too – albeit cheating on her the whole time. So Mia had a soft spot for Jackson. It was clear she didn't hate him, but did she love him more than his money? I took a drag of the cigarette and handed it back to her.

"Anyway, the whole murder is horrible really," I said. "But at the very least you're going to be well taken care of. Jackson was a very successful man. Of course nothing can replace love, but money can help."

Mia laughed again. "You're funny, Kat. I like you."

Why did I feel like the younger one in this conversation? I hurried on.

"I mean, I kind of understand. I lost someone I loved too. Not the same as you, but it hurts...Okay, what are you laughing at?"

Mia was grinning at me like I was a simpleton.

"You and all your love talk. You really believe that

fairytale crap, don't you? Let me tell you something, Kat. Love is for the weak. I hate men. They use you up and treat you like trash."

I nodded. That had been my recent experience with Lance for sure, but I didn't have the loathing she seemed to feel for men in general.

She stubbed out the cigarette angrily against the ground, smooshing it into a pulp until it was unrecognizable. Then she reached in her pocket and I flinched. All this murder stuff was making me jumpy.

Mia withdrew her hand from her pocket and handed me her pack of cigarettes.

"Here. I'm the one that has to quit."

She smiled and patted her tummy. "I'm gonna have a baby. And I'm going to be a great mom, you just watch. I might have messed up a lot of my life, but now I'm going to start fresh. Healthy."

She laughed again sweetly and rubbed her tummy. Then she shifted into the car seat.

Mixed feelings tangled in my chest about Mia. She seemed to love her child but hate men but maybe not Jackson....? I definitely needed to get more answers from her and see what else I could learn that might help Carol.

"Hey, Mia..."I stopped her just as she was about to shut the car door. I acted all chummy. "We're having our first book club meeting at the Landers' Bakery tomorrow night – you should stop by. It's fun."

Mia thought about it. "Maybe. Thanks. I gotta go, Kat."

As she reached to pull the door handle shut on me, I noticed her pale skinny arm had a big *purple whelp of a bruise on the side of it.*

I opened my mouth and it clicked audibly shut when I saw her arm poking free from her jacket.

Bruise?

Like a bruise from an incoming beer bottle cap? Could that be from *my beer bottle cap slinging*? She saw me looking at the black and blue mark, and pulled her coat down over her arm quickly.

I forced my eyes away and blurted out. "It starts at nine o'clock after the Landers' Bakery closes. We'll be having it at the café when it opens..."

She looked me dead in the eye looking for any sign from me. "I'll think about it. If you wouldn't mind moving?"

I scooted out from between her and the door.

She slammed the door shut, twisted the key in the ignition, and pulled away in a hurry. So much for any headway I thought I'd made with girl talk. I was frustrated as I watched her drive away. I took note that she was in a white Mercedes. That seemed like a sleuth thing to do.

****

I felt like Mia had more pieces of the puzzle that would lead us to the real killer but I had blown my cover. If she was the one who chased me, then she knew I hurled that beer cap and it hit somewhere. Enough to elicit a scream, and a bruise.

She wasn't happy I saw it for sure.

But she was also too small. The person who had chased me was larger. But then where did she get that bruise? Could it have been her that chased me that night, perhaps in a big coat to disguise her size?

My conversation with Mia opened up more questions than it answered. She still had the most to gain from Jackson's death, and she seemed to hate men in general.

I wondered if I had just invited Jackson's true murderer to our first book club meeting tomorrow.

CHAPTER 30

I slipped on a nice black dress and hose. I applied some mascara and patted my bangs into submission, which meant dead flat straight covering as much of my forehead as possible. Fie Fuzzbottom for reminding me of the bane of my genetics! I'd gotten my Dad's forehead, and his penchant for a good ale. Would it have been too much to ask for the same French cheekbones my mother had instead? Not that I was complaining. People called me cute.

I applied some lipstick and put on my parka over my pretty dress. (The downside of trying to dress up in a town covered with snow most of the year.) Aphrodite came in and wound herself around my leg. I knew she wanted to come with me, but not tonight kitty. Tonight we had serious business to attend to. We girls were going out on the town to eat some good food, and do some sleuthing. I had gotten the list of competitors from the chili cook off, and had gone down the list. The teams and their corresponding restaurants were listed. Unfortunately, the uniforms they wore were not.

I knew from being a writer/waitress my whole life that most of the teams that had white and black combos were the upscale restaurants. After some research and asking around, we found Six Pines boasted five really high-end restaurants that required their wait staff to dress in the formal black and whites.

Ethel and Summer and I were going to check out each of the restaurants and see if Summer could recognize the man that had given her the note from Jackson the night of the contest.

Ethel picked us both up in the van, again doing the "secret" three beeps. I knew it was going to be one heck of a night when I noticed that Ethel had brought her cane/bat with her. It lay between the two-bucket front seats between the coffee holder and the new café menus.

"Doesn't Earl's grandson want his bat back?" I asked.

Ethel waved it off.

"Can't use that thing until the snow is gone anyway. I'm just borrowing it. He even showed me some of his jiu-jitsu moves with it."

Summer raised an eyebrow at the bat. Ethel had also borrowed the same said grandson's drone Christmas gift to spy on her neighbor, Mrs. Beaverton, during the great recipe theft.

As if reading our minds Ethel said. "I owe that kid a heck of a birthday present."

Summer smiled.

****

We pulled up to the first restaurant, The Great Gatsby. It sported a 1920s theme with old antiques and a cozy dark leather feel inside. Best of all, the wait staff was all dressed in white and black. We looked at each other and shot the thumbs up.

A hostess led us to a lovely table in the middle of the room, which worked to our advantage. Every few minutes, Summer would get up, feigning that she had to go the bathroom because she was five months pregnant now. She would then wander over to different rooms looking for the waiter that may have given her the note.

We planned to order one dish from each restaurant so we weren't loitering. Plus, why not check out the competition's food?

At the Great Gatsby, we ordered potato skins filled with

bacon and cheddar and sour cream. Summer was having a craving, and I was happy to have an excuse to eat fattening food.

Unfortunately, Summer didn't recognize anybody that she remembered at The Great Gatsby.

"Check please," I said to our waiter.

We hopped in the van and headed to the Chilling Station, the next restaurant on our list. It catered to upscale hipsters and beer lovers, and boasted over fifty different kinds of brews. I was excited about this place. The upside of not being able to drive - is being able to drink with your meal! We planned to order salads here, and I had my eye on a dark IPA.

The place was super busy with people lined up at the open bar area. It was modern with clean lines and lots of glass and chrome like someone with OCD had decorated it.

Summer strolled around the restaurant looking for our guy while we ordered drinks.

I perused the menu and stopped when I saw a salad named - *Oprah's Favorite Salad.* How interesting. I read the ingredients that mainly featured lettuce from some place named Mendocino Farms. For the pleasure of having Oprah's Favorite Salad, they wanted $18. Highway robbery!

"Look at this, Ethel!" I exclaimed. "$18 for this salad and all it has in it is lettuce! Not even a darn shrimp or artichoke heart. How in the world can they charge this?" I just had to know.

When the waiter came over, I asked him. "Why is this so expensive – are we paying for Oprah's retirement? There's nothing in this salad but lettuce."

The waiter nodded haughtily. "Yes ma'am, but it's *Mendocino Farms lettuce.*"

First of all, you can take that ma'am thing and stuff it in your uptight pocket. *Humph.* No one should ever refer to any woman as ma'am unless she's over ninety.

"What's so special about Mendocino Farms?"

"Oh ma'am, they sing over all their plants. From the moment they go to seed until the moment they are shipped – daily I might add – the lettuce is sung over like little babes."

I looked at Ethel. This was crazy, but now I just had to have some of that music-raised green salad!

"We'll take one," I said. "And another beer."

Ethel gave me the look.

"What? You're driving and I'm still nursing a broken heart."

Ethel's lip twitched into a tender smile. "Have you heard from him?"

My mouth made a tight line. "Yep. But I don't answer his calls. I'm over it." I raised my hand. "Hey, waiter, do you think I can get another beer here?"

Ethel stirred honey into her chamomile tea. "I can see you're over it."

Summer returned to the table just as the salad was being served.

"Ooooh!" she exclaimed. "Mendocino Farms!"

The waiter nodded. "Then you know about the lettuce?"

Summer beamed. "Of course! I haven't been able to get any of this since I left LA!" She turned to the waiter and they both sang a note in unison *"Ahhhhhhh!"* He smiled at her and said, "Let me know if I can help you."

"What was that all about?" I said when he'd left.

"Heart note. The 'ahhhh' vowel – connects you right here." She touched my chest bone gently.

"Try it, Kat."

I shook my head. No love vowels for me. I did want another beer.

And yes, that darn Oprah salad was wonderful, but still not worth 18$.

****

Summer hadn't recognized anyone at the Chilling Station, so we moved on to the third option on our list.

The next restaurant was on the very outskirts of Six Pines getting closer toward the border of Whispering Willows Village. It was the most prestigious establishment on our list, and where we intended to have our third spying expedition as well as our main course.

The Whispering Pines Supper House was beautiful; it reminded me of the lodge up at Eagles' Peak, only it was a little more elegant with white lace curtains, fancy tables, and an even fancier price tag. Summer smiled. It was by far the most high-status of all the restaurants on our list, and the price reflected that.

"Don't worry, this one's on me, guys," said Summer. Thank goodness for her supermodel cache of cash.

The piece of fish I ordered alone was $58. $58 for a piece of *mahi-mahi* in a green tea reduction served with a beurre blanc citrus sauce and a side of wintergreens.

Maybe that kind of price was acceptable in France, but certainly not acceptable just west of Six Pines. I was kind of relieved that Summer had offered to pick up the check. Until the café opened up, I really didn't have a steady income.

The wait staff was a quick moving sea of black and white. After we ordered, Summer got up to waltz around and do her scouting routine again.

I watched heads turn in her wake as she went. She truly was a beautiful sight to behold, and I could understand how she had made a fortune in the modeling business. True love had brought her back home to Kissing Bridge after all these years - maybe there was still hope for me here too? I sighed and took a sip of my beer.

Summer caught my eye and shook her head dejectedly, as she plopped down delicately on the gold bench outside the bathroom. She hadn't seen anyone she remembered, and now she really did need to use it. She hadn't gotten lucky finding our man, and it seemed we had another failure.

"Is this the only powder room?" Summer asked sweetly to the waiter who was ringing up a check on the computer nearby.

The waiter smiled and turned to her. He was a tall young man with auburn hair and light eyes with extremely long eyelashes. Summer tried to place him.

"Summer Landers!" He beamed in recognition. "I just met you the other day at the cook-off! Remember I asked for your autograph?"

Summer looked and him and gulped. I knew from the

look on her face it had to be *the guy.*

We really hadn't decided whether the letter messenger was part of the murder plot, or even possibly the murderer himself. Summer tucked a hair behind her ear gracefully. "Oh, yeah. I remember. That was a great time at the cook-off."

The waiter continued smiling completely enamored with her. "My name's Brice." He stuck out his hand and pumped hers. "Brice Stevens. So nice to meet you. I just knew you guys were going to win the cook-off - it was ridiculous how many people were at your table."

Summer looked Brice over, and slowly ran one slender hand through her long pale blond hair. Even I was memorized. *Atta girl,* I thought. She was attempting to dazzle him for more information.

"Thank you!" said Summer. "We have some good cooks in our group. We were lucky." Then she added coyly, "Hey, do you remember the note you gave me to give to my Aunt Carol?"

Brice turned his head – one of his tables was signaling him to bring them the check.

He glanced back at Summer and said, "Yeah, I remember. I have to go, sorry – it was great seeing you, Summer."

She reached out and grabbed his hand. "Wait, wait! Did

Jackson give you that note to give to me?"

The waiter pulled his eyes back to Summer. "Who is Jackson?"

Summer blinked, and then tried to contain her surprise. "He's a friend of my aunt's."

"Oh I don't know him. I was just waiting in line to get your autograph and some girl gave it to me and asked me to give it to you for your aunt."

Summer hastened as Brice's manager walked by with a stern look in their direction. "Can you tell me what she looked like?"

Brice reddened at his manager's ire, and hurried on. "Uh, she had a nose ring and was about this big," he held a flat hand out about a foot below himself, "dark hair, lots of eyeliner..."

"Was she wearing a big diamond ring by any chance?" said Summer.

The guy brightened. "Huge! Must have been three carats. Her boyfriend must be loaded. I really gotta go; my boss is eyeing me up."

****

Summer sat back down at the table with us, and shot us a thumbs up low-key. The dinner had been delivered so I was in the middle of my third bite, and it was delicious

I have to tell you. Of course it could have used a little liquor.

Summer recounted what she had learned from the waiter. "I found him! His name is Brice. But, he didn't seem to know Jackson's murder was tied in any manner to the note. He didn't know any of us either - other then we won the blue ribbon, and we had the most people around our table. He just wanted my autograph."

Ethel leaned forward "Are you sure Summer?"

She nodded. "I was looking him right in his eyes, and I can tell you he wasn't lying. I believed him."

We were hanging on her every word.

"He said some thin girl with a nose ring wearing black gave him the letter. He was standing in line to get my autograph, when she approached him, and asked him to pass the note to our table when he got up front." She took a sip of water. "This is the best part - he confirmed she had a *huge diamond ring* on her wedding finger!" She looked back and forth at the two of us. "You know what that means?!"

Ethel and I both said in unison.

"*Mia* was the one who sent the note!"

CHAPTER 31

We dropped off Summer, and Ethel and I let ourselves into the bakery.

We were still wide-awake with thoughts about what we had just learned. Ethel was stressed so she wanted sugar. I always wanted sugar.

The bakery was closed. I absentmindedly grabbed a bottle cap out of my pocket and snapped it at the light switch. It flipped on a low light. Thankfully, Ethel was too busy to notice. She headed straight for the kitchen, and I locked the door behind us.

I decided to start a fire while Ethel pulled together some ingredients in the refrigerator to make a batter for some chocolate mini soufflés. I broke up small branches to add to the fire. I had a feeling we were going to be there for a little while.

"So now we had to put Mia back on the top of our list of suspects for Jackson's murder," I said. "If she gave the letter to be delivered to Carol, she must've known she was planting it. Plus she had that bruise on her arm that could have been my bottle cap."

Ethel looked up from whipping the batter. "How do we know if Mia even read the letter she passed to Brice?"

I blew on the small flame and the kindling sparked into a fire. "Well, I guess it had the seal on it... but it seems kind of odd that his new wife would be giving his ex-fiancée a private correspondence from him so willingly."

Ethel stealthily poured the dark aromatic batter into small singular tin soufflé cups. I could smell the chocolate and I felt some stress leaving my body.

"Ethel - what would Jessica do now?"

Ethel considered it. "She'd stick with the note. The note is missing because *somebody took it.* The police would've been able to prove that Carol was set up if they had the letter from Jackson. That's obviously what Mia didn't want them to know, and why she didn't tell them. But *who is she protecting? Or is she protecting herself?*"

I watched the flames grow in the fireplace as I considered our options. "Well, I invited Mia to the book club tomorrow –if she shows up we can find out for ourselves...Maybe I can get her to open up to me more in the casual setting of a small cozy group?"

Ethel nodded. "Good idea. I'll make something special for your first book club tomorrow Kat."

I smiled. I was looking forward to our very first meeting.

As if on cue, the buzzer rang on the stove, and Ethel pulled out the chocolate soufflés. She set them to the side, as she whipped up some fresh crème in a bowl. I watched it beat until the creamy white liquid finally stiffened enough to be dolloped on the side of our soufflés.

I couldn't get the new knowledge we had learned out of my thoughts. How innocent was the waiter Brice in all this? Why hadn't he come forward right after the killing? Surely he had heard about the murder? Maybe he didn't make the connection with Jackson's seal – but maybe he knew more than we thought. Who knew if he was even telling the truth? He was a stocky guy, he could have very well been the figure in black I saw that night of the murder.

I considered all the evidence as I watched the flames grow a little higher, and added another small log. I dusted off my hands, and walked back over to the counter to take a bite of that delicious soufflé.

We're getting there Aunty Carol, I thought. *Don't lose faith in us.*

CHAPTER 32

The next morning, *without calling me,* Ethel and Summer went in early to the bakery to rustle up some luck - *Landers style.*

Dodie was already in the bakery opening the restaurant and putting the freshly baked delicacies in the front display window, when they both bustled in with guilty looks on their faces.

Ethel had Grandma Izzy's recipe book under her arm, and a determined look on her face. They both waved to Dodie as they beelined straight through the red connecting door, and disappeared into the café. The new equipment for the café had been delivered, and Ethel wanted to try it out before the official opening. At least *that was their excuse.* Dodie never believed them for a minute.

Summer chewed on her lip and watched her mother, Ethel, exploring the new equipment in the back of the cafe.

"Shouldn't we call Kat? She's in the middle of this whole thing as much as we are. Her life could be in danger if she really can identify the real killer."

Ethel shook her head. "Some things are best left to family, dear." She patted Summer's small belly bump.

"You'll learn someday, darling. Family is the only thing you have in the beginning, and in the end. We need to keep this between us – for now."

Summer nodded.

"Did you bring the juniper leaf?" Ethel asked.

Summer patted her stylish Gucci bag. "Yes – it's the last I had, by the way."

"We'll forage more after we get Carol out."

"Okay."

"Did you grind it already?" said Ethel.

"Yes, Mom, of course."

Ethel looked at her sternly. "Not coarse, we need fine."

Summer laughed. "I know, Mom, settle down. I said *of course* I ground it *fine*. Extra fine."

Ethel nodded her approval. She flipped opened Grandma Izzy's recipe book.

"I haven't made this recipe in years..." Ethel squinted at the pages. She flipped through the enormous volumes. "I wonder if it's under appetizers, or T for Tea Sandwiches..."

"What about looking under brunch?" Summer offered.

"Here it is." Ethel's said triumphantly. She ran her finger down the list of ingredients and instructions lovingly.

"These little sandwiches are delicious, actually; they have this pop of surprise in the aftertaste. The juniper leaf when it's ground up has this wild, peppery-fresh accent to balance out the sweet red tomato and basil."

Summer patted her tummy. She was getting hungry. "Sounds wonderful. Have you ever made these for me?"

Ethel laughed. "No, honey. I've never needed to make this sandwich for you. Your nose twitching has given you away since you were a toddler – this is for the *good liars.*"

Summer raised both eyebrows.

"Now Carol and I were a different story. Mom went round and round with us about that broken statue of Elvis she had in the corner. She was always incredibly intuitive, as you know, but she just couldn't seem to find the culprit behind dear plaster Elvis' beheading."

Ethel giggled like a little girl in remembrance. She continued, "Carol and I had been dancing, and Carol had swung me jitterbug style straight into the plaster Elvis in the corner, beheading him in one perfect twirl. When Elvis's head fell off, we were in shock. You can imagine! Carol stuck it back on the body and Elvis's head kind of

177

leaned up against the wall, but other than that, he appeared good as new. *Until,* your Grandma Izzy was vacuuming one day too close to Elvis, and his head rolled off and landed right at her feet..."

Summer's mouth fell open. "No! Grandma Izzy must have flipped out! What happened next?"

Ethel smiled. "Let's just say the whole horrible truth of what really happened to poor plaster Elvis came out *after* she served us these little sandwiches as our afternoon snack at our Sunday *Breakfast at Tiffany's brunch.*"

Summer's mouth flew open in indignation. "Not *at* the *Breakfast at Tiffany's Brunch*?"

Ethel nodded. "I know. It was savage. We never saw it coming. Claimed it was a new recipe she was trying out – and of course us being offspring of the legendary Izzy, we fell for it. After a few of these, and Holly Golightly dealing with her *mean reds,* Carol and I just blurted out the whole sad end of the plastic King of Rock. We both got grounded for two weeks. Kind of harsh, I thought, since it was an accident. But Mom was overly attached to that Elvis. We did get his head stuck back on perfect with Elmer's glue in the end, so why we got grounded I still don't know!?"

Summer narrowed one eye. "So it's one of those

recipes?"

Ethel winked. Summer comprehended.

She came over and looked at the old recipe book with her mother. *"Truthful Tomato Caprese Tea Sandwiches...* So.. these make people tell the truth?" asked Summer.

Ethel nodded. "Oh, yes. After eating one triangle of one of these sandwiches, the truth waterfall just starts flowing. People's secrets just come blabbing out of them with no filter. It's serious stuff. But then these are serious times."

They looked at each other.

"Mom," Summer said, "just who are we making these sandwiches for?"

Ethel grinned.

"I think I'm going to prepare a little appetizer for Kat's book club meeting. Especially for Mia..."

Summer's eyes lit up. Her mother never ceased to amaze her.

Ethel tied on her apron and inspected the new oven they had just put in the Enchanted Café. She nodded her head in approval, and then set it to 350 degrees. She whistled to herself as she pulled out some fresh basil from the new refrigerator and set it on the chopping block on the counter.

Summer tied on her apron and took up the large sharp cutting knife and faced the basil.

"How do you want this, Mom?" she asked.

"Slivered," Ethel said with finality.

CHAPTER 33

Ethel hustled back through the bakery/cafe connection door to grab some fresh tomatoes from the pantry. Dodie eyed her up suspiciously. The Landers' Bakery was stuffed full of town regulars getting their coffee, sweets and breakfast sandwiches. The sandwiches had been Dodie's idea, and actually spawned the need for the full menu café next door.

She, being a natural mother, had worried the skiers needed more sustenance than coffee and a scone to keep them skiing all day. She put together a fabulous breakfast sandwich that was tasty and healthy to keep them stay full of energy all day on the slopes.

The new Landers' breakfast sensation consisted of seven seed bread home baked that day (of course) topped with a very easy egg over, olive oil, kale, fresh mint, feta, fresh ground pepper and pink crystal sea salt, all topped off with a bit of aioli mayo. The breakfast crowd loved it, and ate it up in droves. Ethel and Carol finally named it after it's inventor - *Dodie's Dreamy Day Sandwich*.

Dodie and the Landers had come a long way together.

Ethel thought of spilling the beans to her because she was practically family.

It was that *practically part.*

Some things are better kept secret, and some of those things were magical tea sandwiches to trick the truth out of possible murder suspects!

Ethel grabbed some tomatoes out of the bakery kitchen refrigerator without a word. The crew in the back all echoed hello to their boss, but Ethel just waved distractedly, and kept her attention on picking out the perfect tomatoes. She held each one thoughtfully, looking at the color, and weighing it, and giving each one the final test - a gentle squeeze to test the juice level.

Grandma Izzy's recipe had called for tomatoes that were - *"In the bloom of beauty and perfection..."*

Ethel picked out twelve of the precious tomatoes, and put them in a big blue-checkered bowl, then wandered off back to the café with the goods. The kitchen crew stopped and looked at each other questioningly.

By the time Ethel joined her, Summer had a pile of beautiful thin cut basil sitting in a neat pile. Her mother nodded her approval as she set the bowl of tomatoes down on the counter next to it.

"What kind of bread does the recipe call for Summer?"

Ethel queried.

Summer stood up and went over to Grandma Izzy's recipe book. She read through the recipe ingredients and instructions.

Ethel let out a "Humph."

Summer shrugged.

"What shall we use?"

Ethel thought about it. "If no bread is specified than it's up to the creators' discretion."

When it came to Grandma Izzy's recipe almost always you went by *exactly as she had written.* But often, over the years, the Landers ladies had experimented with her recipes, and added touches of their own, ultimately inventing new favorites that were added to the big book.

Summer thought about it.

"You're the blue ribbon Queen mom! What kind of bread do you think would taste best with the Truthful Tomatoes Caprese Tea Sandwiches?"

Ethel considered. "Hmmm we have fresh pumpernickel for the egg sandwich special today...But, I think I prefer the lightness of the potato bread."

Summer nodded emphatically.

"For sure."

"I just had Dodie teach the girls how to make bread. We have a bunch of the students homemade potato dough already made in the freezer..."

Summer patted her growing belly.

"Hmmm that sounds delicious. I'm ready to eat again."

Ethel smiled lovingly. "Well we're going to get you something right now little mother. " She rubbed Summer's stomach affectionately. "I'll grab you some cauliflower and tarragon soup the girls are making in the back for today's special. How about that and a heaping side of some fresh baked potato bread with some creamy butter?"

Summer smiled. "I'll start slicing the tomatoes."

Ethel ran back quickly again through the bright red connecting door, and grabbed the dough out of the back bakery freezer. This time she wasn't getting by the manager.

Dodie had been taking in all the comings and goings of Ethel through the connecting door, and she knew *for sure* Ethel and Summer weren't at the cafe *just* inspecting the equipment. They were cooking without her!

Dodie stopped Ethel in midstride as she strode through the kitchen. A line was forming at the front counter waiting to order food and buy sweets, but

Dodie needed to talk to Ethel and she wasn't letting her off until she did. "Ethel what's going on over there with you two?"

Ethel hurried by. "Oh hello dear. Just getting some soup for Summer and..."

Dodie was not being put off.

She demanded, "What are you doing with the bread dough? Is something wrong?"

Ethel patted Dodie's hands affectionately. Dodie really was so sweet. "No, no dear. Everything is fine- other than my sisters in jail for a crime she didn't commit. Summer and I are just...well..."

She floundered looking for a suitable fib that Dodie would believe. Dodie knew her pretty darn well.

Dodie put her hands on her hips. "I know you're cooking over there Ethel! I saw the bowl of tomatoes you tried to smuggle by me! Good try."

Ethel was caught red tomato handed.

"Okay it's true! We are, but we're just surprising Kat, and putting together a little appetizer for her first book club meeting tonight! She is so excited about the first meeting and we just wanted to make something special for her to share."

Dodie smiled and looked at the door to the café curiously. "Oh okay. That's real nice of you Ethel."

Ethel faked humility. "Well I try."

With that, the feisty senior turned and beelined through the bright connecting door to the café before Dodie could ask her any more questions.

CHAPTER 34

In no time, they had six fresh loafs of potato bread baking in the oven. Summer had finished her first cup of soup for lunch, and wanted another.

"I'm eating for two," she explained. Ethel waved her into a seat.

"Hush – I'll get you another cup of soup. The first loaves are almost done!"

After another cup of cauliflower soup and three pieces of fresh potato bread, the Landers were ready to get down to serious gourmet business.

Ethel drizzled the sliced tomatoes with a balsamic vinegar reduction, and then popped them into the roasting oven to broil for exactly two minutes. Just a little heat to pop and bring out their sweetness, she said, but not too much to lose the fresh tanginess.

The potato bread was sliced thin, so as to not overpower the flavors between them. The authentic Italian Caprese cheese had been torn by hand – as per the recipe's order. Everything was almost ready for assembly. The oven rang, indicating the tomatoes were done, and Ethel popped the tray of bursting beauties out of the oven.

"Oooh, that color red with the tinge of blood garnet! It's scintillatingly superb! Summer," Ethel cooed, "did you know that color –"

"– *and presentation is 80% of the joy of eating food,*" Summer recited.

They both laughed. Summer had been raised by food legends and heard this famous mantra since birth.

Ethel took out a spatula and tenderly scooped up each tomato from the rack, then put them on a silver platter. She brought them over to the counter and set them down.

"I think we're ready..." Ethel turned to Summer with a gleam in her eyes. "Now where is that ground juniper leaf?"

Summer withdrew a velvet pouch from her purse.

"You wanted the juniper leaf collected on the harvest full moon, right?"

Ethel nodded. "Of course darling."

CHAPTER 33

The Cozy Book Club met once a month on the full moon. It seemed a fitting time for a club meeting at the new Enchanted Cozy Café, but since it wasn't yet open, the bakery would do.

Tonight was just the first organization meeting to plan out objectives. I was thrilled to be the group's leader, elected because I was a writer, and, frankly, the most excited about it.

Ethel had promised to make us some delicious secret appetizer for our first meeting.

My best friend, Elle, came early to help set up. She was elated to get a night off from the lodge to spend with me. I put the CLOSED sign up on the bakery and locked the door until the other members would arrive.

Elle and I popped some beers and sat down at the new counter. I pocketed the caps in my back left hip pocket, as usual.

"Feels good in here," Elle said with a grin.

Tonight Elle had her flaming red hair up in two side

ponytails. She didn't look old enough to be allowed to drink beer.

"Yeah," I agreed, looking around the place. "I can't wait until this horrible mess is settled so we can open up and get back to normal."

Elle raised an eyebrow over one emerald green eye. "Speaking of normal, how are you doing, Kat? Is your heart still in there, or did you throw it off into the Seine before you got on the plane to come back home?"

I smiled. Elle knew me better than anyone. "It's been tough. But I think I'm getting over him. Jerk."

Elle shook her head. "What was he thinking?"

"I don't know."

I opened the new double-sided café fridge to get another beer. I had been at the café day and night, overseeing all the construction, decorating, new menu item selection, and helping with the specials. I kept my own private stock back here in the café fridge because it was empty, and because I was pretty much in charge of the place until we opened officially. Then I would be the head night waitress, or, as I liked to refer to myself – *night manager.*

I noticed a couple trays of sandwiches in the fridge as well, which must have been the secret appetizer meant for the book club. Ethel was so sweet.

I peeked under the aluminum foil. Caprese sandwiches. Yummy.

With a little shuffle, I pulled out the top tray and Elle helped to arrange them on a pretty red and white flowered plate. Elle sampled one of the sandwiches that were cut in triangle shapes and a look of love melted over her face as she tilted back her head. "These are to die for!"

Oooh, how I now loathed that phrase. "That good, huh?"

She nodded emphatically and popped another into her mouth.

"Amazing. Man, those Landers can cook."

She had it right there.

I picked one up and took a bite.

Gosh darn, it *was* incredible. How did they do it?

Elle munched away happily as I pushed a couple tables together near the fireplace where everyone in the club would sit.

"I think that Frankie guy might be sick or something." Elle said after a moment. I stopped and turned to face her.

"Why would you say that?"

"The maid found a bunch of syringes in his garbage, and she reported it to me," said Elle. "I asked Helena about it – obviously we can't have illicit drugs in the suites, and she told me it was for his medicine."

A glimpse of the syringe I saw in Frankie's coat pocket came to mind. Maybe he had some illness – or maybe that was a lie his mother told to protect him.

"Anyway," Elle continued, "they have all their bags packed in both their suites so it looks like they're on their way out. They've run up quite the bill. I hope the rumors aren't true."

My head shot up. "What rumors?"

Elle nibbled on her sandwich delicately. "I heard that they are near penniless. All the pomp and circumstance is for show. That's why they came. To get her inheritance back from Jackson."

I sucked in my breath. So Jackson was right. They had come to Kissing Bridge needing money. If Frankie was sick, then maybe they needed that money desperately.

Perhaps *desperate enough to kill.*

I put the beautiful triangle cut tea sandwiches and some small bright yellow plates in the center of the wooden table. Then I started on the tea.

I took a big glass carafe and added ice. We already had brewed lemon tea in the back fridge. I added that and some heaping scoops of honey. I finished it all off with fresh sprigs of mint I took straight off the plant growing next to the cashier.

We were all prepared. I snapped a bottle cap off the picture of George Washington on the wall and it boomeranged off and hit the lock mechanism on the front door of the bakery, switching it to open.

I was ready for our first book club.

CHAPTER 34

It was a small group of cozy book readers that turned up for the first official meeting.

Mostly we just planned to pick out the books we were going to read over the next three months so everyone could purchase them and get reading. Ethel and Summer were exhausted, so they had gone home to their husbands earlier that day. Dodie had to open the bakery in the early morning – so it was just me and Elle and the book club members. Oh, and Aphrodite of course.

I pulled her off my neck and warned her she was going home if she misbehaved. There were fifteen people in all, and we were all acquainted as Kissing Bridge locals usually are.

I was a bit disconcerted and surprised when Brice Stevens, the waiter from Six Pines, showed up. I wondered how he knew about a book club in Kissing Bridge? Maybe Summer had mentioned it. He seemed to have a super fan crush on her. Maybe he had hoped to see her again.

"Hey, Brice." I greeted him warmly. Brice smiled. "I

didn't know you were a book lover."

His warm eyes matched his smile. "Yeah, I love books! Thought I'd check it out."

I wasn't sure I was buying his story.

"So, what did the police have to say when you reported what you knew about the letter – and Mia? Because nothing has changed. Carol's still in jail."

Brice rubbed his auburn hair and shuffled his feet. "Yeah, I'm sorry I haven't had a chance to go by and give my report yet. I've been working every day until tonight."

But you still had time to go to a book club in a city not even close to you? I thought. Hmmm.

"Is Summer going to be here tonight?" Brice asked.

I shook my head. "Gee, no, sorry. She's home in bed. Her condition, you know."

He nodded, though obviously disappointed. "Sure, she's got to take care of herself."

"Anyway – take a seat we are just about to get started."

He went over and joined the others that had already taken a seat at the table. I looked over at Brice Stevens, the stranger, amongst all these people I knew well. Was

I putting them in danger? Who knew if he was somehow involved in this murder? Why hadn't he come forth sooner with news about the letter to Carol that might have helped solve the case? For all I knew, he and Mia were involved in this together. They *were* both from Six Pines.

And he had the body type I was looking for.

Other than Brice, whom I still hadn't decided was safe; I liked the mix of young and old in the group. Everyone *ooohed* at having a snack, and we all munched the sandwiches between conversation. Aphrodite curled up in the middle of the long wooden table, and she let everyone take turns petting her like she was royalty. Which, unofficially, she is.

After some more noshing and debate, we decided on one murder mystery – how apropos – one romance book, and one thriller for our lineup. We'd gone through two rounds of sweet tea and three plates of sandwiches when things got a little strange.

Chuck Darling, a young local electrician, started talking about how he had purposely lied to his dad about getting a scholarship to MIT because he didn't want to leave his hometown.

Dolly Madison Adams, the local realtor/elf who owned the store down at the corner, patted Chuck's hand to comfort him, and then broke out in tears herself saying how she had forgotten to go to confession at St. Marks' last week.

To add to these odd disclosures, Elle suddenly stood up and confessed, "I took Lightning out yesterday, and I know Dayton wouldn't approve, so I fibbed to him and told him I took Sunshine instead."

The group murmured their understanding. Lightning was an ex-racehorse that everyone knew was crazy. Dolly soothed her now that she had stopped crying herself. "Well, you didn't want to upset your husband – it's understandable." The book crowd nodded, supported, and concurred as one.

I smiled from ear to ear. I had no idea that this book club would be such a loving, supporting, and giving group! I knew a book club would be a fun way to share and enjoy reading together, but the camaraderie I was feeling and the deep connection going on was something I never counted on! It was like *free group therapy.*

As I nibbled on my sandwich, I felt the love and safety of my new book comrades with every delicious bite.

"My boyfriend fake married me!" I suddenly inappropriately blurted out between bites. The book club members all stopped talking and looked at me at once. I immediately regretted my intimate personal information blab out.

Amanda Sweeting, the local librarian, five foot tall, 250lbs with a dark black bob and bright hazel eyes, waved off my concern from over-sharing.

"We all heard, honey."

At my confused look, the entire book club burst out in unison, "Your dad told me at the pub."

Everyone laughed at themselves for saying things in synchronicity, and also for having had the *exact same conversation with my father.*

I wasn't laughing. Really, Dad?

Oh, well. At least I didn't have to worry about the news of my fake marriage getting around.

I saw Brice happily chewing on a sandwich and not for the first time that night I wondered what he was really doing here at our book club, and what the heck was under his shirt? I had already surreptitiously examined all his outer extremities that were exposed and not seen one suspicious mark. Those extremities were very nice, I might add. But I really wanted to see his chest. I needed to see if Brice had any *wounds or a bruise from my bottle cap bullet.* And I was suddenly feeling very unfiltered – even for me.

"Hey Brice," I called across the table. "I'd love it if you took your shirt off."

Brice's face brightened as the table turned to look at him. He pointed to himself. "You want me to take my shirt off – ?" He stammered. "N-Now?"

I nodded emphatically.

"You have no idea how much."

He looked around the table.

Amanda raised her eyebrow at me. "Well, I never tried that technique," she said. "Do you spank him later?"

"Spank? No!" I shook my head. I needed to see that body for altruistic reasons only.

"I really want to check out your body, Brice, I mean it," I continued truthfully.

Echoes of, "Me too! Me too!" rose up from around the table.

Brice smiled. "I like you Kissing Bridge book readers, you're a wild lot. I always wanted to try this."

With that, Brice leapt onto the center of the table and commenced with a simulated strip tease dance by slowly removing his shirt and waving it above his head. He then pulled it in and out between his outstretched legs.

Dolly pulled out some singles.

The book club was loving it, but all the dancing was

making it harder for me to see if I could spot my bottle cap mark on his body.

At about ten o'clock, Maxine slipped in the back door of the kitchen and snuck up on me as I was pleading with Brice to put his shirt back on again. I had thoroughly examined him, along with everyone else, and I had seen not a mark or fleck on his perfect physique.

I jumped in the air when Maxine whispered in my ear, "I would have closed up earlier if I knew the book club was going to be so interesting."

"Hey – oh, Maxine! How's it going, Max?" I hugged her. Tonight she was dressed in a long, full-length gold sequin coat à la Elton John with a pink furry boa around her neck. She had topped off this outfit with a powder pink wig and long fake eyelashes that had sparkles at the tips.

Max had promised to stop by for the first meeting, and I couldn't help but be relieved to see her. Maxine was a good egg. Strange dresser, but a true down to Earth person I could trust.

She took my hand tenderly and looked in my eyes. "Seriously darling, I heard you've been going through some hard things around here with Carol being accused of all this nonsense," said Maxine. "I just wanted to let you know I'm here if you need me."

I impulsively hugged her.

I hadn't gotten any time to catch up with Maxine since the murder; it was comforting to be talking to her. "Yeah, it totally stinks."

"Hang in there, darling." She hugged me again tighter. "Things will get better."

The book club members still whistled and clapped at Brice. The side of Max's mouth lifted in a smile.

"I'm so glad you came to the meeting, Maxi. Come sit down and have a treat. We..."

"Well actually, darling, I just came by to warn you."

My eyes went wide. Uh oh...

Maxine took my hand and pulled me out of the back door. She pointed down the alley between our shops and towards the Henderson's' Wine and Cheese store, *Wino's*, across the street.

"I've been watching Jackson Jennings' sister, *Helena* – I think it is –from my door. She's been over at the wine and cheese shop quite a while. She's gone through every wine sample they have and the last of the Henderson's goodwill. I saw they were trying to close up, but she didn't seem to be in a good way. She was ranting about some box... Anyway, I locked up for the night quick and just wanted to let you know. I last saw her hobbling this way in her pearls and Chanel."

My violet eyes widened like a cat in the dark. Helena? What was she doing here on Main Street? It's not far from the lodge, but it was a heavy, stormy night. I had been relieved to see so many people make it to the first book club meeting – but they were sturdy Kissing Bridge locals and used to bad weather.

I wondered where her Harvard clone unsociable son was.

Maxine kissed me on the cheek and grabbed one of the triangular sandwiches from the plate I still held in my hand and hadn't served.

"Gotta go, I've got a date. Good luck."

"You too," I said.

She winked as she slipped out the back door.

I wasn't sure I could deal with any more sleuthing tonight, but it looked like I didn't have a choice.

I looked up, and spotted Helena's dizzy head poking in the front door waving a wine bottle in her hand.

"Got an opener?" She yelled across the bakery.

CHAPTER 35

The wind whipped in a big blast of snow through the open front door and sent a chill through the room. Aphrodite *meowed* her irritation at having her comfort level altered.

I got up to shut the door behind Helena and went to retrieve a wine opener before she yelled again.

The now sedate group of book lovers stopped chatting amongst themselves and looked up at the newcomer.

Helena wasn't just tipsy. Helena was trashed.

I was thinking she must've had some bottle of something hard in her bag, because no amount of wine could do that to a person. I crossed the room quickly to help her to a seat, because she almost fell straight on her face, and I'm pretty sure that would've been a really nasty lawsuit that the Landers wouldn't have appreciated.

I guided Helena to a counter chair, and she pretty much collapsed onto it. I gave the club table the silent *I don't know what's up* sign with my shoulders, then grabbed some of the teacakes from the platter and brought them over to the drunk in the chair. One thing I've learned in life is that if somebody's drunk – feed them.

So I offered Helena some food.

Helena looked at the tea sandwiches and then motioned for me to open the wine for her with the wine opener as if I was her personal servant.

I popped it and went to look for a glass, but she had already tipped it back and was drinking straight from the bottle before I located one. So much for elegance when you're already trashed.

It was getting late and the book club group was starting to file out.

Helena continued to drink, ranting like a madwoman under her breath as the book club members shouldered past her, trying not to stare. She nibbled on a sandwich and nodded her approval. I was looking forward to getting some answers out of Helena, especially now that she had some alcoholic truth serum going for her.

I also wondered if I should phone Jaime and let him know she was here. I didn't trust anyone these days, and she was in a rare state. Could she have been like this and killed her brother in a drunken rage? I was happy to see Brice leaving alongside Dolly, chatting about some place in Borneo he hoped to go to.

He stopped on the way out. "Hey, I forgot to mention this

to you. I don't know if it matters, but that girl who handed me the letter the other night – before she came over to me, I saw her talking to some guy by the back door."

I stepped closer. "What kind of guy? Could you recognize him?"

Brice shook his head. "No, I didn't see his face, just the back of him. But he was wearing all black – black hat too. I don't know if that's helpful, but I just remembered."

Helpful? He had no idea.

I thanked him and hugged Dolly goodbye.

So – *a man in black handed Mia the letter*. That was very interesting indeed! For now, Brice was off my list.

I followed the last of the book crowd to the front door and waved goodbye. "See you all next month!"

I turned back to my unwanted intruder. Helena looked really upset. Her eyes were red and puffy. I guessed she'd been crying. I was happy to see her take another big bite of the Caprese sandwich because she sure needed to sober up.

She shook her head oddly, as if she didn't know which way to shake it.

"Can you believe it? Can you really believe it?" She

ranted on and on after I closed the door.

Actually, after what I'd been through in the last few days, I could just about believe *anything*. In this case, I had no idea what she was talking about.

"Believe what?" I said.

"He left it all to her! He left all our family money to a lying, scheming child out of spite."

"Excuse me?" I said.

"The will, the will!" Helena snapped her fingers. "The big reading was today. Mr. Maritime all beside himself because Jackson left him nothing but some stale cigars. I got something that was already mine to begin with – and she got all my family's oil money!"

The will....

Oh goodness, I had forgotten all about the reading of Jackson's will today! I forced myself to stay on track now that Helena's filter was obviously way off.

I was trying hard to understand. As I said, I'm not a brilliant girl. No one thought I was going to college, if you know what I mean. I struggled to comprehend her drunken ranting and learn more.

"So Jackson's will was read today?" I said as I plopped down next to her and popped open a beer. "What happened?"

Helena cackled. It sounded like she was doing an imitation of the evil witch of the east on purpose.

"We got *screwed* – little Kat O'Hara with your big violet eyes and your little boy body, and not in a good way."

Little boy body?

I glanced down at my less than prominent bust. I always chose to think of myself as athletic. Even though I'm not.

Helena tipped the wine bottle back with more force, and I prayed she wouldn't chip a tooth on the glass. Or maybe she ought to.

"Oh, I'm so sorry," I feigned. "That's not right."

She swung the bottle at me like a pirate. "Exactly! You know that's not his baby, don't you? Mia with her supposed pregnancy – ha! Jackson had a vasectomy years ago; he never wanted to have children. But did he even put that stipulation in the will? NO! He just left her all OUR money without even the condition of a DNA test to make sure it was his baby! But the worst – the worst..."

Helena broke down and started crying, and I actually felt sorry for her. Whatever happened, it certainly seemed as if Helena was a victim in all of this too. And where was her son? He certainly couldn't be happy knowing that his inheritance and school college fund had been stolen from him.

Not for the first time, I also noted that Frankie was the same size as the man that I had seen crouching by Jackson's house that night. The same man that should be wearing a remembrance from my beer bottle cap.

Plus, Elle had said they were packed and ready to leave the lodge.

Helene's crying seceded, and she settled down enough to take another bite of her sandwich. She chewed for a while and seemed to relax and open up.

She slugged down some more wine and sighed. "At least I finally got my music box. I don't even care about the darn painting. I just wanted to help my son. You don't have kids do you, Kat?"

"Just five cats."

She nodded. "Not the same, but still you'd do just about anything to help them, right?"

I nodded. I glanced at Aphrodite giving me the evil eye in the corner because I refused to let her back on my neck.

Helena suddenly reached into her purse and pulled out

an exquisite silver music box. She wound it up on the bottom and set it down carefully between us on the counter. It was a treasure of an item, inlaid with silver scrolls and what looked like fairies playing on the top. From its depths, the music player lilted out the notes of *Edelweiss* in a haunting tinny sound. It looked very old, and very expensive.

"It's beautiful," I said.

"This is what Jackson left me in his will," she stated as she gazed at it with nostalgia.

I didn't understand if she was happy or sad about it.

"Do you like it?"

Her eyes lit up. "Like it? I love it! My mother gave it to me when I made my first Holy Communion when I was just eight years old. It was passed down from my grandmother, to my mother, and then to me. It's very special to me."

I completely identified with Helena at that moment. I had a locket my mother had given me as a child and it meant the world to me. It's odd how it can be the little things that mean so much after someone you love has passed.

Helena slugged back some more of her wine, and wound up the music box for another round. "This is what I was looking for when I saw you in the house on Six Pines the day after Jackson died." She said as she examined it lovingly, turning it over and running her fingertips along the silver. "All these years Jackson hid it from me. I think he was jealous of me getting such a beautiful item at such a young age." She shrugged her aquiline shoulders in a haughty gesture. "I begged him to return it to me after Mom died, but he refused to give it to me – and then I get it like this."

I could feel her pain. "I'm so sorry you got it through your brothers' passing...at least your mom would be happy knowing you finally have it now."

"True," she said thoughtfully, "but she would have been much happier knowing that the miniature Picasso painting that was attached to the inside was still there."

CHAPTER 36

Picasso. I gaped at Helena. *The* Picasso?

Helena flipped open the music box to show me the red velvet lined inside where one might keep rings or valuables, and on the inside cover was a frame with a piece of glass. Behind the glass was a picture of Jackson at a young age. Even as a toddler, he had shock white hair. In the picture, he looked like he'd just had a tantrum and was sticking his tongue out.

Helena laughed. "This is what I found in place of the painting that was there. Even from the grave, he mocks me. I had hoped to sell that Picasso – the one that used to be behind this glass. It was an original. My grandmother modeled for him when she was in college in Madrid." Helena smiled slightly at the memory. "She was quite a woman, my grandmother. Anyway, I had hoped to help...to help Frankie."

She looked at me and I had a glimpse of the beauty she must have been before time, and a tough life, had worn her down.

I didn't trust Helena, but right now I believed what she

was saying.

She took another swig of wine and continued talking as she gazed at the music box.

"I never cared about money. When I found out Jackson had suddenly struck oil on our homestead – after tricking me into selling my half – I really wasn't bitter. I was an artist. I didn't care about money. It never seemed to make my parents happy. I just needed enough to care for Frankie and me after his father left us."

She traced her finger along the top of the music box. "I hid this in my bedroom behind the sidewall when I left home, but as usual, my brother was one step ahead of me."

I couldn't believe what I was hearing. "He stole your Picasso and switched it out for a picture of himself?"

Helena nodded.

"Sick sense of humor." She looked up and smiled at me. "Been that way since he was a child. Money was Jackson's only real love. Sadly, he took after my father that way. That's why my mom was so adamant when she gave me this. I didn't understand what it was worth then, but she made me swear to keep it hidden for a rainy day. When I found out Frankie was sick, I knew I had to come back to the house and get it so I could sell the painting and pay the medical bills. But Jackson got to it first."

We looked at the picture of Jackson with his bratty pucker. She suddenly snapped it shut, as if to block out his memory.

I got another bottle of beer and returned to the counter and sat back down with Helena. I looked at the elegant silver music box as the music slowly faded and finally died. For a while, we both just looked at it and didn't say anything. I drank my beer, and she slugged her wine.

Jackson hadn't just stolen her family fortune; he'd taken the only thing Helena had to pay for her son's medical bills, whatever they were. Despite my sympathy for her situation, it still made her and her son my top suspects. Not only was Frankie big enough to be my unknown assailant – but now I knew he was also fighting for his life.

CHAPTER 37

I jumped when the front door to the bakery banged open. Frankie burst in sans his Harvard uniform. Tonight he was dressed all in black. Black. All black like the man I saw in black? Where were all the Harvard regalia clothes now? Maybe that was all a good guy act.

He looked flustered and red in the face as if he'd been drinking – possibly a family problem. After the reading of the will and the loss of his future, perhaps he wasn't taking things very well.

Aphrodite let out a howl I had never heard from her before and jumped off the table and back onto my neck.

Frankie barely looked at me as he grabbed his mom roughly by the arm. "Come on, Mom, let's go."

Helena reluctantly set the wine bottle down, replaced her music box into her bag, and allowed her son to lead her out the door. A cab was waiting with the lights on at the curb. As I shut the door behind them, I heard Frankie say to Helena, "We're leaving tonight. I hate what this is doing to us, Mom. I'd kill him again, if he weren't already dead. I swear it."

Chills went up my body at the hatred in Frankie's tone.

What did he just say?

***

There was a knock at the back door, and I jumped.

Gosh darn it, now what? I wasn't feeling like dealing with any more people.

The person rapped again on the door, and called out. "Kat you in there? Its me open up."

I let out a sigh of relief and opened the door.

It was Jaime, in his Kissing Bridge deputy uniform. I was really happy to see him. He looked around the empty bakery. Aphrodite lifted a paw as if to say hello. I gave her the eye, and she slinked off and sat down in a chair and scowled at me.

Jaime did a quick check in the back kitchen, and bathroom, and then tried the door lock between the café and the bakery. "Mom said one of her clients was getting out of control, and she thought I might need to escort her back to the Lodge. She thought she was headed this way?"

Jaime's parents owned *Wino's* across the street. Wine and cheese for discriminating tastes. I motioned toward the front door.

"Helena was here. I could have used you a few minutes ago, but her son came and got her and they just left in a cab. She was a wreck. Guess Jackson made a big joke of things in his will – left Mr. Maritime some old cigars, and he left his sister a music box that he'd hid from her all these years– but when she opened it, he had switched out an expensive original Picasso inside for a horrible photo of himself instead! It was an awful thing to do. I felt sorry for her.... She said that Jackson left all his money to Mia. She's going to be one rich twenty year old."

Jaime shook his head.

"Was going to be a rich twenty year old."

I looked at him trying to register what he was saying.

"I'm sorry Kat, but I just came from Six Pines. They found Mia's car, and well.... She's dead Kat."

I gasped and brought my hand to my mouth.

"Oh no! Poor Mia!"

I couldn't get the thought of just seeing her so alive and ready to be a mother, and now she was dead. I sat down and put my hands in my head. Mia dead. Another death – and her so young, and her baby...It was horrible. Aphrodite came and curled up next to me as if she felt my sadness.

I continued to take deep breaths trying to calm down and find some kind of center in all this. We didn't have these issues in Kissing Bridge. The only calls to the police had to do with cats in the trees and such travesties. Not death. The oven timer dinged for the quiche I'd put in during the meeting, but I ignored it.

Jamie paused. He glanced at the oven. "Aren't you going to get that?"

It was nearing midnight, but I had slipped in a quiche to bake to surprise the opening crew tomorrow so they would have a special treat when they came in before the busy day. Things had been tough with Carol gone, and we were all trying to do little extra loving things when we could to help keep our strength up, and get us through this difficult ordeal.

I pulled out the creamy quiche from the oven, and checked the side. The crust was the perfect shade of gold and brown, and there was just a touch of crinkle on the top so I knew it was done all the way through. I loved making quiches because you could throw almost anything in pastry with eggs and it would taste awesome. This one included broccoli, Brie cheese, pancetta, roasted garlic, and of course a touch of liquor *a la French style*. Again, I'm sticking with the dark beer for the perfect accent flavor. I'm on a run here.

I served it up to Jamie with a cup of coffee and watched as he gobbled it down. His blonde surfer locks were sticking out of his deputy hat all askew and his shirt looked like it was choking him at the neck.

He finally loosened his shirt, and I could see his muscled pecs pressing up against his white T-shirt underneath. Jaime was looking extra good to me right now.

Jaime had certainly matured *well* since high school, when we dated. I remembered him as *super athletic,* and really passionate about watching skiing and doing stunts. When he took up snowboarding, he was one of the first ones to do the big pipe tricks.

I couldn't help but smile just a bit, thinking about us back in high school, and now back here together again.

The news about Mia was horribly sad and upsetting, but it was still nice to have Jamie here as company after everything that had happened. Jaime had always had a way of making me feel better when things were bad, and we went back a long way. If I had to come home to Kissing Bridge heartbroken and penniless, at least Jamie Henderson was the silver lining in my cloud.

I considered telling him how I was feeling about him. There was this overwhelming state of wellness and safety that made me believe I could just open up and share all that was going on with me.

Aphrodite sauntered over and sat on a chair by us at the counter. She stared at us intently. *This was not an innocent look.* I've come to know Aphrodite, and she's not named after the goddess of love for nothing.

Then she took it upon herself to leap off her chair and plant herself in Jaime's lap, pointing her paw at me. How uncouth! I had to teach that girl some tact. I picked her up quickly before Jamie wondered what the heck was going on with my weird cat. She wrapped herself around my neck again, refusing to be put down. Fine.

Jaime glanced at my live fur cloak but he neglected to say anything and kept eating his quiche. For that, I have to give him a lot of credit. Props to you for knowing when to keep your mouth shut buddy. I liked that in a guy. Heck, I like that quality in anybody because I'm nothing like it. Whenever I want to say something, it just blurts out like a cork from a champagne bottle.

Something ached in me to get close to Jaime. Talk about old times and forget all about this murder business. I hadn't even heard if he liked his new job as a deputy, or if he was seriously dating anybody. I refilled coffee and poured in some of the warm cream with just a bit of Bailey's in it that I had on the stove. He was off of work, after all.

After the second helping of quiche, I still couldn't get the thought of my conversation with Mia out of my head. Her determination to quit smoking and her smiling face at her future as a good mother....

It was all so heartbreaking.

"I need to know the details about Mia's death," I finally said. "I thought she might be on her way here tonight. I invited her to the book club."

Jaime's beautiful green eyes seemed to dive into my violet ones. Suddenly, I didn't want to talk about murder – but I had to know.

"How did it happen, Jamie?" My voice was low. "Car accident?"

Jamie looked up and shook his head. "It doesn't look natural, and it doesn't look like an accident."

My eyebrows shot straight up like arrows. "You're saying you think Mia was murdered too? Tonight?"

"Coroner put the time of death at 20:30– I mean, 8:30 PM, but we won't know until we get the full autopsy back tomorrow. I can tell you one thing, her name wasn't Mia and she wasn't pregnant. She went to a lot of trouble to disguise herself with that fake baby bump. In any case, she had a bunch of suitcases packed like she was leaving town."

I got up and walked around the room. Mia murdered? And faking her pregnancy too?

I told Jamie about what I heard Frankie say, but thinking about it now I realized it may have just been an expression, the way Dad threatens to kill me if I drink his last Guinness. Jamie chewed slower as I spoke and said he'd mentally file that information away.

"Do you think the same person killed Jackson and Mia?" I said. "Even if what he said was a figure of speech, I just can't help thinking that Frankie has the most to lose in this. I think you should find out what he did all night before he picked up his mother."

Jamie looked at me with a little smirk. "It does seem logical. You're getting pretty good at this, Kat."

"Yeah, well, Ethel's the expert..."

Jaime raised an eyebrow. "Your seventy-something boss is the murder expert?"

I corrected him. "*Murder She Wrote* expert. Take it from me; no crime school could have been better training." I laughed. "She's our secret weapon."

Jaime laughed too. It was a deep, authentic sound that made me realize again why I had liked him so much. Unlike Lance the poser, Jaime was just himself. A Kissing Bridge Mountain local that loved the land and his family.

Lance with his big city dreams and lost hometown values seemed like a ridiculous choice for me now. I don't know what I ever saw in him. I shook Lance out of my head, and focused on Jaime's beautiful green eyes.

"Gee, you have really pretty eyes, Jaime. Like emerald gem colored."

Jaime chuckled. "You been drinking, Kat? I don't think I've ever heard you give me a compliment."

I blushed. "That wasn't a compliment, Jaime Henderson."

He was smiling like a Cheshire cat – or Aphrodite, who was purring like a Ferrari engine right now.

"Sounded like a compliment to me..." He shoveled another bite of the quiche into his mouth.

"That was an observation."

He looked up. "Right. I think you're sweet on me, Kat, admit it."

I felt blood rush to my cheeks. Good grief, now I was going to blush like a teenager in love? I stamped my foot like a little girl. This was not going the way I liked it. I pulled a bottle cap out of my pocket and shot it across the room in irritation. It banged off the stone fireplace, hit the coat rack in the corner, and turned off the main overhead lights. At least I could hide my embarrassment with some low lighting.

The fire crackled and I made a big to-do of acting like it needed another log on it, when in reality I just wanted to not be looking at Jaime Henderson right now. But he seemed to gaze right through me.

I tossed another log on the fire and prodded it around with the steel poker.

Then I cleared my throat and refocused. Carol was still in jail, and I had a mission bigger than my own ego. For once.

"So how was she killed?" I asked again.

Jamie patted his mouth with a napkin. "It looks like she was strangled by one of her own fishnet stockings."

I gasped.

"Unlike Jackson's," Jamie went on, "this looks more like it could've been passion driven."

"What does that mean – *passion driven*? For the amateur sleuth here, can you take it slow?"

Jamie had to laugh at me. "You're so darn cute, Kat. The way things come flying out of your mouth. You're so real."

I shrugged.

I came back over to the table and took a bite of the quiche left on Jaime's plate. It was good, if I do say so myself.

"Kat, you know Carol well. She had a relationship with Jackson before she married the doctor. Mia had bruises all over her body. Do you know if Jackson was abusive?"

I thought back to her in the car and the bruise I had seen. "I saw a bruise on her arm the other day, but I thought maybe it was from my bottle cap. I thought she might have been the attacker that night in a disguise. Do you think the bruises were made by her killer?" I questioned.

"It looks like some of them may have been new, but by the looks of them – many were older. In other words – somebody's been abusing that girl for a while."

My eyes widened. "Do you think it was Jackson?"

"Well, he would've been at the top of the list, but he's dead. Since these bruises are new, I'm thinking possibly the murderer knew Mia better than we think, and she was holding out on us. I think she knew exactly who killed Jackson, and she decided to take the money and run."

"I remember I was talking to her, and when I saw the bruise, she wasn't happy about it."

Jamie reached over and took my hand. I remembered Mr. Maritime at the window of the café screaming into the phone. Had he been looking for Jackson? Jackson and his group showed up shortly after he had been looking in the café window. I told this to Jamie too.

"Mr. Maritime... I don't know how he's involved, but he might have a part in this." I shuddered as I realized that Mr. Maritime fit my mysterious attacker in black as well.

"Helena was drunk, but she said that he had been expecting money too in Jackson's will. That he was really upset because Jackson left them nothing but joke gifts and cigars and all his money went to Mia. Maybe someone should be interviewing him?"

"Kat, let's go down to the police in Six Pines and tell them everything you suspect tomorrow," said Jamie. "Right now let me take you home. Lock your door. I know it's Kissing Bridge, and I know you've got your dad there so I don't have to worry about you – but I don't want to see anything happen to you."

I relented and let Jamie drive me home. It was late at night, and I really was freaked out by the whole second murder in our small town area. Somewhere out there, somebody was capable of multiple murders. I hoped and prayed that this was the last one.

CHAPTER 38

The next morning I woke up and I couldn't get the idea of Mr. Maritime being involved out of my head. I hadn't spoken to his daughter, Diana, in quite a while. I thought it might be a good idea to invite her to coffee and sweets at the bakery.

Diana Maritime was more than happy to come meet me at the bakery for lunch. Her youngest had just started Kindergarten, and she had a joie de vivre about having an hour to herself where she could actually talk with an adult and have a great meal.

I sat Diana down at a small table by the sundries case that held the jams and homemade jellies. I brought over some coffee and cream then scooted behind the bakery window to grab some goodies.

Ethel looked at me sideways from her post in the

kitchen.

I made sure Diana was comfortable, and went over to have a chat with Ethel. We were all still pretty shook up over the news of Mia's murder. I filled Ethel in on who Diana was, and how I hoped to get some more information out of her regarding her father's part in all of this.

Ethel's eyes lit up and she told me she had something perfect for our lunch. She scooted away so quickly I didn't have a chance to tell her about my encounter with Jackson's sister last night.

Ethel sprinted like an Olympian around the corner, and in through the connecting doors leading to the café. She was digging through the refrigerator urgently, when Dodie followed her into the café kitchen.

Ethel tossed ingredients onto the table haphazardly.

Dodie looked at her questioningly. "Ethel, are you all right?"

Ethel murmured with her head still stuck in the refrigerator. "Hmm I made these tea sandwiches for the club last night but I hid some extra just in case I needed them for a special lunch... But, I can't seem to find them...?"

Dodie's face got red. "They weren't Caprese tea

sandwiches were they?"

Ethel's head nearly snapped off as she leapt out of the interior of the refrigerator. "Yes!"

At Dodie's crestfallen look Ethel started to moan.

Dodie threw her hands up in the air. "You said you made them for the club you didn't say to save any... I gave the leftovers to the staff for their employee lunch special..."

Ethel moaned. "They were *special alright*."

Dodie started pacing back and forth.

"I'm sorry Ethel."

Ethel stopped her.

"It's okay sweetie. No harm done. And they did their job already so..."

Dodie stopped in her tracks. "What do you mean by special?"

Ethel rocked her head back and forth. The gig was up, she'd have to tell Dodie the truth. "Like they *were special...from my mother Izzy's book*." Ethel put a finger to her nose like the Godfather.

Dodie's eyes widened in understanding. "Oh – *that special.*" She grabbed Ethel's hand and ran back through the connecting door to the bakery with her.

"I don't think anyone's taken their break yet to eat we've been so busy all morning! Maybe we can save them!"

Dodie hustled through the busy bakery kitchen and to the back refrigerator and threw open the door. A look of joy came over her face. "Here they are." She said turning to Ethel. "Not a whole lot left – but some!" Dodie pulled out a tray with the last of the tea sandwiches covered in plastic.

Ethel grinned. "Some is just enough." She took the tray delicately out of Dodie's hands. "I'll just take care of them. Maybe you can serve the chicken salad special to the crew instead?" She winked.

Dodie nodded. "Good idea."

Ethel resurfaced at our table, flushed, and over smiling. She put down a lovely red flowered plate with the Caprese sandwiches I recognized from last night. I wasn't in the mood for veggies, and really was hankering for the Sloppy Joe on special today, but Ethel gave me the evil look when I opened up my mouth and went to refuse her offering.

I fake smiled back and said, "HMMMMM. Thanks Ethel how kind."

She nodded in agreement with how kind she was, and stood at the table loitering and staring at Diana. I had no idea what she was up to.

Diana picked up a triangle and tried a nibble. "Delicious!" She beamed. "So unusual – that woodsy taste..."

"Pine pepper." Ethel said flatly.

Diana's eyebrows shot up.

"Really, pine pepper? I've never heard of that before where..."

Ethel cut her off. "Glad you like it – go ahead finish up I don't want to interrupt hungry ladies."

She laughed in a strange sinister way, and then hurried off. I turned to see her hiding behind the back kitchen divider spying on us. I decided to let Diana eat her full, and concentrate on how best to illicit the information I needed out of her without it sounding too forced.

Diana Maritime had strawberry blonde hair and bright saucer sized hazel eyes. Her face was cherubic round, like her father's, and even at thirty she looked like a little kid ready to do something bad.

For the first half hour we reminisced, and I listened to the difficulties of new motherhood and a husband who works two jobs. It was hard but they were happy. I asked about her mom and dad and she hesitated. I knew I had my in.

I leaned forward. "What's going on – your mom and dad are in good health aren't they?"

Diana was pulling on her lip with her two front teeth like she always did when she was going to lie, *or fib,* as she used to say. I stopped her.

"I've known you our whole lives Diana – what's going on? You can tell me."

Diana abruptly broke down and started crying loudly.

Customers looked over at us concerned, and Ethel gave me the eye. I patted her hand; I guess she was just tired of holding it in. The ear of a caring – *albeit also self serving in the name of Aunt Carol friend* – was what she needed, and the floodgates of emotion had let loose.

She dotted at her eyes with her red napkin. "They invested all their money in a oil project with Jackson Jennings. My dad had brought him the deal, and Jackson had the equipment, and at first it was great. I mean they made a lot of money. But Jackson kept putting my dad off about paying him back his investment - let alone the profits. Then the house got foreclosed and Jackson stopped returning dad's calls... and then he was murdered."

She looked up at me. "Now he's dead so there's no

chance of getting any of my father's investment back let alone the profit. They lost the house I grew up in – and all he left my poor dad was some stupid box of Cuban cigars and my dad doesn't even smoke!"

I felt so bad for Diana. I had shared so many good times with her family in that home on the hill. I felt her pain.

But I was also worried that her father may be the new top suspect in Jackson's murder.

****

Ethel came over to see how things were going, and I mentioned how Mr. Maritime had just read the will. Ethel tried to remain casual as she leaned against our table.

"How are you enjoying the sandwiches, darling?" she cooed.

"Oh they are to die for, Ethel!" Diana said as she munched away happily. "My dad would be so jealous – these Caprese sandwiches are his absolute favorite."

The hair on my arms stood up.

I had been looking for a reason to talk to Mr. Maritime in person to see what I could find out.

Ethel was way ahead of me. She grabbed the Caprese sandwich from off of my plate that I hadn't touched, and made a big to do about wrapping it up.

"Well, Kat," she said, drippingly sweet, "didn't you mention we had to go right by Beacon Park this afternoon?"

I raised a brow. Ethel continued.

"Well that's right by your father's office, isn't it, Diana?" said Ethel.

Diana nodded, still shoving the sandwich into her mouth gleefully. "Yeah he's right there in the Halston Building."

"Well, isn't that coincidental." Ethel said. She grabbed my sleeve and pulled on it. "Kat, why don't I wrap this up and we'll just drop this off for him. Everyone's had such a terrible time of things and all."

Diana nodded. "Thanks he'd love that!"

CHAPTER 39

E thel and I packed into the van and started down the mountain and towards Mr. Maritime's law office.

"So what's going on with those sandwiches, Ethel? I saw you ready to bust a gut when you found out Dodie was about to serve the rest of them up to the employees."

Ethel glanced at me but remained silent.

"Give it up. I'm your partner. I'm on a need to know basis, and right now – I need to know!"

Ethel looked in the rear view mirror then glanced at me again. "Let's just say they are *special*."

I wasn't settling for that.

"Special – how *special*?" I pressed.

She glanced at me again quickly, and then focused back on the road. "Special, as in maybe they make you want to tell the truth, the whole truth, and nothing but the truth..."

She made a big pretext about examining the street signs she'd seen a zillion times. I was done with this mumbo jumbo. Trying to solve these darn murders was enough for my simple mind.

"Gosh darn it, Ethel, can you just tell me the truth?"

She glanced at me unsure of how I might take the truth.

I waited.

She finally let out a loud sigh. "Okay. Okay. They're *Truthful* Tomato Caprese sandwiches...From my mother Izzy's recipe book?"

I waited. Again – simple mind here.

Ethel looked at me like I was a dunce. "One of her *special recipes*..." She touched her nose again like the Godfather.

My eyes widened.

Was I actually hearing what I thought I was? "Are you saying those sandwiches are magical? Like all the rumors about you Landers ladies are true, and you actually did some kind of hocus pocus with the food?"

Ethel waved her hand delicately at me as if batting at a butterfly. "Careful darling. That's harsh. They've hung innocent people throughout history with that kind of talk. We prefer – *herbal medicine*."

Humph. I don't remember any herb making me blab out the truth when I didn't intend to. Maybe an alcoholic herb? Hops?

I thought back to last night and blushed.

"Oh my goodness! That's why the book club was so bizarre last night." I brought my hand to my mouth and gasped in remembrance. I turned to Ethel and said accusingly, "I made Brice take his shirt off, and I may or may not have made a pass at my old boyfriend!"

She shrugged. "You got some great information out of Helena though."

Now how could I argue with that? Darn it Ethel.

CHAPTER 40

The outer offices of Maritime and Squell were all lined with deep cherry wood bookshelves filled with impressive looking law books. The floor was sleek and marbled. The furniture was modern, and the ceiling was adorned with cylindrical chrome lights. Ethel and I sat down on the expensive Italian white couch. It was super uncomfortable, but it looked really good.

After a few minutes, Mr. Maritime's secretary called our names, and escorted us inside his office. Mr. Maritime got up from his desk, and shook both our hands.

"To what do I owe the pleasure ladies?" He asked.

I began, "Diane was over at the bakery today, and she said that Caprese sandwiches were your favorite, and it was the last of the specials today so..."

I nudged Ethel.

That was her cue to hold out the bag. Mr. Maritime looked at us, and I continued on. "We were passing by, and thought how nice it would be if we stopped by and dropped the sandwich off for you."

His eyes lit up and he looked at the brown paper bag in Ethel's outstretched hand. "Caprese? Hmmm that is my weakness. Do you mind?" He said withdrawing the wrapped sandwich from the bag.

Ethel waved her hand like she was on the rose parade float giving a peasant a favor. "No go right ahead that's why we brought it for you."

"So you could get it while it was... fresh..." I finished weakly.

Mr. Maritime was a portly man and I could see we had made points by bringing him food. He unwrapped the sandwich and his eyes lit up. "This looks delicious and I haven't eaten all day."

Ethel and I were looking good. "Go ahead and eat some," Ethel cajoled.

Mr. Maritime looked at the bag longingly.

"No, no, no! That would be rude to you ladies. I don't want to take up your time watching me eat. Now why are you here exactly?"

Ethel kept pushing the Caprese. "Please eat Mr. Maritime! You'll offend me if you don't. I worked really hard on that special."

"Well then, if I must." Mr. Maritime shrugged, and smiled

as he unwrapped the sandwich. "How very thoughtful of you both."

We smiled, and waited.

He took a big bite and chewed. Almost immediately his affect seemed to change, and he relaxed and smiled as he continued eating away contentedly.

Ethel had the grace to wait until he swallowed, and then she pounced. "We're wondering if you think that Helena or her son might have had a reason to kill Jackson?"

Maritime made a clearing sound with his throat like he was uncomfortable, and then he got up and locked the door to his big office, and came back and sat down.

He groaned when he fell down into his seat again, and motioned for us to take the two seats across from him.

"Listen ladies, I've known you a long time. Kat, I've known you since you were a little girl. I don't know what's going on, but there's something strange happening. I mean, other than the murder of Jackson and him lying in a bunch of chili. That was beyond horrible... but the last few days I saw him before he died, he seemed very edgy, and that wasn't like Jackson. We hadn't always seen eye to eye, but it's not like Jackson to back out on a business deal. He's the one that insisted we add the provision to his will to make sure that I was repaid my investment in case of his death and that his sister would be sure to inherit his fortune. Then the other day, he and Mia show up together at my office, and he hands me a sealed document, wax insignia and all. Seems he had gone and written up a whole new will!"

Ethel and I looked at each other.

"I didn't open it, but then I didn't expect he was going to be murdered either – or that he would take out the provision where he paid me back what he owed me!"

He continued to chew while Ethel and I scrutinized him.

"I lost everything. I had all my money tied up in my business with him and now there doesn't seem to be any documentation I can locate that protects me. That's what he left me instead."

Maritime pointed to a box of cigars in the middle of his bookshelf that ran floor to ceiling. "I've never had a smoke in my life. My dad died of lung cancer."

He shook his head. "The ultimate blow. He really had me fooled. I had thought we were friends at one time. Helena wasn't much happier with the music box Jackson left her either. In fact, she appeared almost traumatized when she opened it up and something seemed to be missing."

Mr. Maritime lifted his napkin to his mouth, and sighed,

recalling the scene. "Helena kept saying there was something very important that was missing, and that it was very expensive. I'll tell you what though, *Mia seemed very interested in that.* In fact, she looked like she wanted to snatch that music box right out of Helena's hands! As if she hadn't already stolen their whole inheritance..."

He suddenly glanced at the clock and stood up.

"I'm so sorry, ladies – I just noticed the time. I have an appointment in a few minutes. We're going to have to wrap this up. Thank you so very much for the wonderful sandwich. I'm definitely going to come to the grand opening of the café if you're serving food like this."

Ethel snorted. "Of course we're going to be serving food like this. We're the Landers, for goodness sake."

Maritime led us to the door. I rushed to ask one more question. "Mr. Maritime, do you think that Mia had any reason to be afraid of Jackson?"

He made a funny face. "If anything, he was afraid of *her*. I would check up on that girl. I don't think she's quite what she seems. She would be my top suspect."

Mr. Maritime obviously hadn't heard about Mia being murdered. Either that or he was playing us. He had said it himself that he had lost his fortune because of Jackson.

As much as I hated to consider it, maybe he was just trying to point the blame towards someone else.

I glanced back at him intently studying some papers on his desk, preparing for his next meeting, as we let ourselves out.

"Mr. Maritime..." I said, as I pulled the door shut behind us. "Mia is dead."

CHAPTER 41

We went back to the café and shut the door behind us. The good news was they were releasing Carol; the bad news of course was it was because Mia was murdered while Carol was in captivity. Fuzzbottom had interviewed Brice and Summer about the letter. But *the letter itself* was still missing. Still, it was good enough evidence to clear Carol and allow her to make bail, and go home.

Our dear Aunty Carol was now safely home (needless to say she *took to the bed*), but she still remained a suspect in the murder. Worst of all, the real murderer was still roaming free, and our main suspect was dead.

We had to figure out a new plan of action. That required chocolate, according to Ethel. Who was I to say no?

Ethel grabbed a bowl, some cocoa, honey, cinnamon, and some brandy. Gosh darn it. So Ethel already knew my *French liquor trick*! So much for my handicap.

She started whipping everything together in a frenzy. "Okay, Jessica usually goes over all the evidence at this point. Grab the notebook."

I pulled out our sleuthing notebook from my purse, and took a seat at a counter chair. I looked over our notes and added a few items we had recently learned. Ethel set the timer on the oven and slipped the chocolate batter into some soufflé tins.

She wiped her brow and cocked her head in thought. "There's got to be a connection between the man you saw lurking around Jackson's house and *both of the murders*. I don't think we can rule out Mia as Jackson's murderer just because she was a victim herself. Jaime told you that she had been wearing a fake pregnancy pad – well maybe she could also have disguised herself to resemble a big man?"

I shook my head. "I considered that too when I saw the bruise on her arm initially. I thought for certain it proved she had been the person I hit, but that wasn't the only mark. According to Jaime, she was covered in bruises..."

Ethel popped the tins into the oven. The aroma of deep chocolate wafted up and enveloped me.

I thought back to my conversation with Mia outside the lodge. "When I talked to her the other day, she really didn't have any love lost for men. But I also don't think Jackson was the one hitting her either."

Ethel pursed her lips. "Yeah, he's not much bigger than

Mia. She probably could have beaten him up. He was 85, for darn's sake."

"So who *was* responsible for the black and blue marks all over her body?"

We looked at each other. Mia was being abused by someone. She also had faked a pregnancy and had been the biggest beneficiary of Jackson's death.

"Jaime also said she had suitcases in the car – as if she were leaving town."

Ethel washed her hands. "Maybe Mia was murdered because she was planning on running, but whoever killed Jackson wasn't about to let her get away with all his money."

I thought about it. "And he's the man wearing my bottle cap mark?"

Ethel shrugged. She finished up with the dishes as I filled in all the smaller details from what Jaime had told me about Mia's murder and my open discussion with Helena last night. Thanks to Ethel's *special sandwiches*, Helena had really spilled the beans.

I thought back to Frankie and his black attire. Something wasn't right there either. Helena and Frankie had gotten the raw end of the deal for certain, as did Mr. Maritime. They all had motives. The thing that confused me was why Mia would want to kill Jackson. As his wife she would have been rich anyway, and old man Jackson couldn't live forever. Did she really need to kill him? Not as much as Frankie wanted to go to Harvard, I bet.

That syringe in Frankie's pocket still hadn't been fully explained. Brice had said Mia and some *unknown man in black* had been talking before the note was passed to Carol. The question was, did Mia know the man in black, or was she just an innocent messenger, as Brice seemed to be? Now I'd never be able to ask her.

Ethel dolloped fresh whipped cream onto the top of the mini soufflés and served us each a plate. As if reading my mind, she said, "I think we need to find out more about Mia and what her life was like before she showed up in Kissing Bridge."

I agreed.

We did need to find out more about the mysterious dead woman that no one had ever seen in Kissing Bridge until the big church upheaval. Mia had mentioned she lived in Six Pines...

"So..." Ethel continued as she tried a bite of the soufflé and seemed satisfied. "We need to find out where Mia lived and go search around her place and see what we can find. That's what Jessica would do."

It looked like another breaking and entering was in order. "I'll bring my bat/cane." Ethel said with finality.

I nodded.

I liked Ethel's enthusiasm, and I liked the cut of her mettle. I was starting to think that this senior was even more rebellious than I was. Not to mention one heck of a cook. I ate the chocolate soufflé, and life seemed good for a minute.

CHAPTER 42

Ethel picked me up the next day at my house with her signature three rapid beeps, which was our new official spy code, and I trudged through the snow and jumped in the side seat of the van.

For some reason, Ethel had decided to wear the flounciest blue gingham dress that *poofed* out all over the place and barely fit in her front bucket seat. I was in jeans, and a sweatshirt – *appropriately dressed for sleuthing.*

"What's with the dress?" I asked, as I opened the hot air vent on my side of the van so it blew straight on me. I had my parka and extra snow gear tucked away in my backpack just in case. I pulled my knit cap down further over my big head. I didn't know where our adventures might lead us today and it was only supposed to get colder.

Ethel shrugged. "Just wanted to look nice for Earl later."

I raised an eyebrow and kept my mouth shut. *But, I'm pretty sure Jessica Fletcher never went breaking and entering in that kind of girly outfit.*

We drove down the mountain carefully. The snow was picking up again and it was nearly white out conditions. We were going to Six Pines bent on finding out something that would give us more information about Mia. I had googled her name, but come up with nothing about Mia Jennings.

If that was even her real name.

Mia's car, the white Mercedes she'd been in the day I talked to her up at the lodge, was registered to Jackson, and had his address. I also hadn't been able to locate any *legal proof* of Mia and Jackson's supposed marriage. Finally we got lucky after I did a quick social search. I located a coffee place called *Nevens' Coffee Heaven* that was all the rage with the black garbed gothic crowd. Maybe Mia had frequented Nevens' as well?

Ethel and I had a plan. We were going to divide and conquer. Ethel was going to go to Nevens' Coffee Heaven and ask some questions.

Since we didn't have any other real leads, we just figured Ethel could hang out and do her nosey old lady act, and maybe we'd get lucky.

Since I had encountered Brice, Helena, and Frankie last night, I was going to go in and give my report at the Six Pines' Police Station. After my research, it seemed Helena and Frankie really had been duped by Jackson, thus giving them motive, and making them my new top suspects.

I had looked up an old article in the Six Pines' newspaper about the oil they had discovered under the Jennings' land. I found it odd that Helena had sold her part of their family home to Jackson – right before the oil was found. Perhaps Jackson neglected to tell his sister that the family lot had a whole pile of oil under it - *until she had signed off on the house?* It was a horrible thing to do to your own sister, but it would make Helena's hatred of her brother more understandable.

I also needed to share my sad suspicions about Mr. Maritime and Brice. I didn't want to be right; I just wanted the police to lift the charges from Aunty Carol. I also wanted to suggest a possible forced body check of Mr. Harvard and Mr. Maritime for any telltale marks from my bottle cap.

They were both the same size as the creeper I saw at the scene, and present at the same time Jackson was murdered. I started up the stairs to the police station, armed with all our theories of who the real crockpot killer was, and my bottle caps, of course.

CHAPTER 43

I wish I had Ethel's job. Although I did worry she might be getting socially rejected by the cool goth kids at the ultra-trendy coffer bar with her Little Bo Peep outfit on. At least she was getting a fresh ground brew, a tasty pastry, and antisocial rhetoric.

I ended up with Fuzzbottom.

Did this guy ever get off work? He seemed lost in his own world, when they let me into his office he was looking at a photo. I caught a glimpse of a younger version of him with his arm around a happy looking girl, smiling from ear to ear. Did Fuzzbottom have feelings? He tossed the photo into his drawer and looked at me like I was a piece of dirt, as he motioned for me to sit down with one hairy hand.

Once again I found myself across from the Wolf-man of

Six Pine's. Of course Fuzzbottom didn't like me. Maybe it was the way I couldn't help staring at his overly hairy neck, or my penchant for tipsy donut moves in a blizzard? Whatever it was, he barely listened to anything I had to report and instead looked up at the clock with an irritated wince every few minutes.

I couldn't believe it! Fuzzbottom obviously wasn't taking our detective work seriously! I wasn't really sure how to emphasize the colossal skill that Ethel embodied. She was a *Murder She Wrote expert.* That meant she was an *expert.*

"Anyway," I continued, "*someone* has my bottle cap mark on them – you find them and I'm pretty sure you find the killer. How's the hunt for that man in black going?"

Fuzzbottom's eyes glazed over. He was in an extra foul mood even for him.

"It's quitting time for me, lady. I've got your story; I'll make sure it gets passed on and we question *your suspects.*"

He frowned as he stood up and strode over to the coat rack. He grabbed his coat, and opened the door and held it open for me. I guess that was my signal to go. I was confused, as usual.

Flustered, I got to my feet and stammered out, "Are you

taking any of this seriously? We have two dead bodies and..."

He grunted in answer, and pushed me forward and out of his office. "Trust me we'll look into it."

"Wait!" I exclaimed. "You need to find the guy with my bottle cap mark. Both Frankie and Mr. Maritime are the size of the..."

But Fuzzbottom wasn't listening. He strongly guided me forward toward the exit of the building. I tried to dig my heels in and stop, but my snow boots skidded on the smooth tile floor.

Fuzzbottom continued to push/slide me further down the hall despite my complaints. "I have all I need to know from you Big Head. You're lucky that guy didn't want to press charges against you. I checked him out, he had an alibi."

Alibi? They had found the man that attacked me? Jackson's possible killer?!

I stuck out my hands like a little kid and grabbed at the side of the walls to slow my exit. "But – who – the knife...." I needed to know. Fuzzbottom continued to push, and I wondered how much more info I could get out of him before...

I was, standing smack in the middle of the freezing

parking lot *outside the police station*. The snow had stopped, but the temperature was way below freezing. There was ice everywhere. I looked around the dark parking lot and the empty streets. I didn't even have a car. I'd have to call Ethel.

I watched as Fuzzbottom walked to his dingy looking maroon Ford Escort. He opened the trunk and rooted around, then opened a cigarette case and stuffed a cigarette in his mouth. He looked back at me looking at him and slammed the trunk down with finality.

I turned away quickly so he wouldn't see my face. A flash of the photo he had held in his hand earlier came to my mind. I recognized that sweet gap toothed smile from somewhere... yes, the hair was lighter, and there was no goth make-up to hide her freckled face, but I was sure...

I froze as Fuzzbottom's car pulled up close to me. He drove past me, and I could feel his piercing brown eyes stabbing into me.

And I knew that black cigarette case.

It was *Mia's.*

CHAPTER 44

I fumbled in my purse, faking a search for my keys as I watched Fuzzbottom through my periphery pull out of the station parking lot and drive away. I looked back to make sure he had made the turn off Six Pines Alley, and then I ran my little butt back into the police station.

I sprinted to the front desk and demanded to see Captain Sykes. After a bit of arguing with the officer at the front desk, Captain Sykes stuck his head out of an office in the back and made his way towards me.

"What's going on?" he demanded of his officer.

"She wants to know the schedule for our crew on the night of the Jennings' murder."

The Captain faced me squarely. I could see he remembered me from being a friend of Ethel's – but he didn't seem too thrilled to see me again.

"Why are you asking?"

I let out my breath. "With all due respect, sir, I think I know who murdered Jackson, and Mia too – I just need to know for certain. Was Det. Fuzzbottom on formal duty the night of Jackson's murder?"

The Captain looked at me earnestly, and then nodded to his sergeant. "Look up the schedule for last week, and let me know if Fuzzbottom was on the schedule last Saturday."

The officer punched things into the computer at his desk. "Nope. He was off."

The Captain looked at me. "Does that help you?"

I nodded. "Yes, Sir. You see, Det. Fuzzbottom is the officer that showed up on the scene, *right after the murder*. He wasn't on duty, but he was in full uniform. And he was there in *seconds.*

"He couldn't have any other officers poking around the crime scene because he had to make sure he covered up his tracks. Mia and he must have written the note to Carol so she could be framed. I'm guessing by the time he booked Carol Landers back here at the station, he was back in his normal street clothes. If I'm not mistaken – that would be *all black except for a red entry bracelet proving he was at cook-off chili contest the night of the murder*. That's why this murder hasn't been solved Captain. My account of the attacker didn't matter to him – *because he was the attacker all along*."

The Captain called out to one of the officers seated in the

back on a computer. He was faking as if he were working because he almost fell off his chair when he was addressed. "Waterman, check the intake pictures from the night they brought in Carol Landers."

"Yes, sir."

The Captain went back and took a look at the screen. He glanced at me, and I knew I was right. He came back and ushered me into his office.

I continued to tell the Captain everything Ethel and I had discovered. Fuzzbottom was the crockpot killer. He had also murdered his girlfriend – Mia. I told him to check the photo in his desk, and he would see that the smiling, redheaded, all-American girl that was arm and arm with Fuzzbottom *was Mia*. With the exact same telltale gap in her teeth.

They were in it together, only something must have gone wrong and he murdered her too. "If you send cars now to pick up Fuzzbottom, you'll find him with not only Mia's cigarette case, but, if I'm right – he also has my signature branding of a bottle cap wound on him that would prove he was the man in black I saw at the scene of Jackson's murder. The same man that tried to attack me."

I told him how I kept going back to the scene of the crime, as Ethel kept reminding me was Jessica's motto.

It was all right there.

Carol holding the crockpot – the perfect suspect. Jaime coming in with me, and then Fuzzbottom suddenly appearing.

When Fuzzbottom ordered Jaime around to get the evidence bag, he made a big deal of taking the crockpot *himself* out of Carol's hands. Of course that would have put *his fingerprints on the crockpot as well – the perfect cover up for his prints that were already on the murder weapon.*

My story must have sounded crazy to the Captain, but it must have also made sense. He got on the phone right away and made some calls and told me to wait out front where it was more comfortable.

Meanwhile, I called Ethel on my cell and told her the mission was off and she needed to stay low until we could get her over to the police station safely. She was all hyped up on caffeine and conspiracy theories and I had to talk her down from a debate going on around her about Monsanto taking over the farming industry. It sounded like she was agreeing to be a speaker at the protest with the goth kids.

"Ethel. Ethel!" I yelled in the phone to get her attention over the loud music. She came back to the phone.

"Hey, I like this place, Kat! Do you want me to pick you up at the station and bring you back here? GREAT COFFEE. Sooo gnarly."

I rolled my eyes. I knew I should have gone to Nevens' instead of her.

"Listen Ethel. It was Fuzzbottom, Ethel. He was Mia's boyfriend for years. I saw a picture of them together. They planned this whole thing. That whole goth attire was just an act to cover up her true self. To lure Jackson and murder him for his money. Only Mia must have decided to take the money and run. Fuzzbottom found her before she could go – and murdered her. He had her cigarette case. Listen, Ethel – he's out there, and he's onto us. Stay put and I'll have the officers come over and pick you up."

But Ethel was already waving goodbye to her new friends and on the road, pumped up on double espressos and adrenaline. "I'm on my way."

I didn't like the thought of Ethel being on the road in her jacked up condition, and with Fuzzbottom loose. Who knew where Fuzzbottom was now, or if he still had murder on his mind?

CHAPTER 45

Fuzzbottom had pulled his car off the main road, and hidden it behind a wooded area, waited, and listened. He had seen the look in my eyes and knew I had figured out the truth about the murders. He had his police radiophone on when he heard the order go out over the wire to look for him; he also heard that Ethel was on her way via Pine Ave.

Fuzzbottom peeled out of his parking spot and headed up the pass to Pine Avenue to get to her first. He cruised to the top of the hill, just out of sight of the main road, and blocked the barren street with his car. He pulled out his mobile light unit and slapped it on top of his Escort so he looked like a policeman on duty.

The bakery van rolled to a stop at the icy pass. Ethel rolled down her window to address the policeman, assuming we had sent an officer to pick her up.

But it was Fuzzbottom.

He ran toward the van bent on grabbing Ethel. He reached for her through the window. Ethel grabbed the window handle and rolled and rolled the knob trying to close the window as fast as she was able - then reached to lock the door - but Fuzzbottom was faster! He grabbed the handle quicker than the senior could lock it even hyped up on coffee as she was.

Fuzzbottom pulled on the door handle from the outside to open it, and Ethel pulled the door handle from the inside trying to keep it closed. Ultimately, his strength won out over her adrenaline, and with a final thrust - he yanked the door handle so hard that Ethel came catapulting out of the driver's seat and landed on the ground ten feet away, all piled up in her blue gingham dress.

Fuzzbottom decided his best bet at this point was a hostage, so he ran over to retrieve the old lady and force her into his car. He tried to get a hold of Ethel's arms as she flailed around with gusto and attempted to free herself of her dress. He finally managed to hook one delicate arm in his grasp.

"Get off me!" Ethel screamed.

Fuzzbottom dragged her along towards his car, but she went limp. Ethel hung on his hairy arm, and she trailed her feet as if both her ankles were broken.

"Wait – I can't walk. I need my cane." She moaned like an old lady.

Fuzzbottom glanced at the van door. He considered getting the cane for the poor old woman, and then decided it would be quicker to just throw her over his shoulder. He turned to hoist her up, and that's when the mighty senior struck. Ethel's cane/bat had been in her dress the whole time. There had been a method to her voluminous dress madness, other than sheer style after all.

Ethel swung her cane/bat like Joe DiMaggio, and hit that Fuzzbottom square in the jaw. He teetered for a moment, and then fell over unconscious like a big furry lump in the snow.

When the police arrived, Ethel was still standing over Fuzzbottom's inert body. She was shaking her head. "Season 3, Episode 7 – 'The Lady in the Blue Dress.' I was counting on you to *not* be a *Murder She Wrote* fan."

CHAPTER 46

Ten minutes later, Ethel arrived at the police station in the van with a full police escort. They had Fuzzbottom in cuffs in the back of another squad car.

I ran to Ethel and clung to her tightly. She hugged me back.

"It's okay, sweetheart," she said.

"Oh, Ethel. I'm so glad you're okay."

I hugged her tighter and she pulled away and smiled at me.

"I told you that cane/bat was a good idea."

I shook my head. "It's a baseball bat, Ethel. You didn't fool anyone with that cane bit."

"Humph." She tossed her head like the baking royalty she was. "Fooled him, and that's all I needed."

I laughed out loud. She had me there.

Captain Sykes came out from the back offices of the station and motioned us to follow him. He handed me a photo he had just printed out.

"The boys just sent me this. Thought you might like to see it."

He showed me the picture. It was a shot of Fuzzbottom's hairy stomach with a two-inch patch near the naval *now shaved*, with a distinct round-rimmed bottle cap wound branded on it.

I looked up at the Captain.

"That's my beer bottle cap mark."

He nodded.

"Looks like you ladies caught our killer. Maybe you can give my crew some lessons." He looked around at the officers – they all put their heads down. It was never good when the bad guy was one of your own.

The Captain walked us out to the van, and assured us all charges against Carol would be dropped.

He did ask Ethel to surrender her cane/bat though.

CHAPTER 47

The grand opening of the Enchanted Cozy Café was a smashing hit.

Everybody agreed they might've had the best time they've ever had at a party. People showed up, young and old in Kissing Bridge to celebrate their famous blue ribbon winning ladies, and of course everybody couldn't wait to see the new Enchanted Café and try the food.

I spotted Mr. Maritime, his wife, and all three of the triplets with their broods in tow. Mr. Maritime was smiling again. He caught me looking at him and made a beeline in my direction.

"I want to thank you, Kat. Thanks to you, everything has been set right."

Maritime's eyes gleamed soft and happy, and there was

not a smidgeon left of the angry, upset man I had seen outside the café that evening.

"Oh, Mr. Maritime," I said. "I'm just glad it's all through."

Maritime shifted his weight. "Well, Kat, I discovered some things that I wanted to share with you since you've had such a big part in setting things right. I have an old law school buddy that is representing Fuzzbottom's case. He said that Fuzzbottom confessed everything, hoping to get a more lenient sentence. Seems he and Mia had been watching old Jackson by himself with all that money for a long time. They hatched a plan to have Mia seduce him, and try and get some of his money. They never meant to kill Jackson – but when Helena and Frankie came on the scene and started making waves about wanting money, Fuzzbottom decided they couldn't wait for the old man to die as originally planned. Mia knew Jackson was alone at his house getting cigars *and that he still carried a torch for Carol Landers.* It was the perfect opportunity to frame someone else for the murder."

My eyes went wide. "So they kidnapped Carol's crockpot so they could get her over to Jackson's house to be framed?"

Maritime nodded. "Fuzzbottom used his police jimmy to get into the Landers' bakery van and steal Carol's crockpot, and then Mia gave Jackson's fake love letter to a random man to pass over to Carol, only *after Fuzzbottom did the horrible deed.*"

It all made sense to me now. "And that's when I saw him trying to creep back to his car to change out of his black murderer's outfit and into his police uniform? "

Maritime nodded. "He hadn't counted on anyone being outside during the announcements of the big prize winners."

That made sense. I wouldn't have been out there myself if I hadn't been sneaking a smoke. "So he had to come after me to shut me up?"

Maritime nodded. "Exactly. But you thwarted him, thank-fully."

I gulped, thinking how close I had come to being one of Fuzzbottom's victims.

"Then when Mia inherited all the money and tried to leave him, he went crazy and killed the only person he ever loved. They might have gotten away with it too, if it wasn't for you, Kat."

I shivered as the last of the details of the sordid story fell into place. I couldn't wait to tell Ethel the whole story now that Mr. Maritime had filled in the last pieces of the puzzle.

I watched Ethel darting about like Husain Bolt with two serving trays of hors d'oeurves for the guests. She was all smiles. She and Carol had insisted on making all the appetizers and they were stunning. Ethel had a tray of tiny lobster dainties with fresh dill and capers in one hand, and a tray of deviled eggs with truffle sauce and blackened shrimp in the other. Earl was beside her with a tray of champagne flutes.

Maybe the fancy expensive Whispering Pines Supper House where we had found Brice had influenced Ethel just a bit. I had to smile when I saw Brice and Dolly come through the crowd hand in hand. I could see Dolly blushing from across the room. I was happy to see them together.

Maxine sauntered in behind them. She was wearing a bright red feather mini dress. She sported an obnoxious orange wig and a new man on her arm. Maxine waved to me and I waved back. I couldn't wait to get her story. But right now, I had one last question for Mr. Maritime.

I couldn't help but think about all that oil money of Jackson's that had been the cause of so much strife. I glanced at Helena and Frankie as they walked around the café chatting with neighbors as if they'd lived in Kissing Bridge their whole lives. Now that I knew the truth, I felt extra bad for them. They had really gotten a rotten deal. I wondered what would happen to them.

"What will happen to all of Mr. Jennings's millions now?" I asked.

The side of Mr. Maritime's mouth lifted up in a smirk at my question. "Well, I finally got smart and opened those darn cigars."

I nodded in understanding. "For sure sometimes a good smoke just makes everything better," I said.

Mr. Maritime looked at me oddly. "Well no, dear, I didn't plan on smoking. I had an idea. You see, I was so mad at that old coot for changing his will and never even telling me. Always pushing me around, never listening to my input, selling our business out from under me. Well, on top of everything, the ultimate hypocrisy – leaving me his Cuban cigars. I was so angry."

He shook his head and then laughed. "You think someone I had known forty years would know I don't even smoke! And then it dawned on me...

When they pinned the murder on Fuzzbottom and Mia, I got to thinking. Jackson was a smart man; he certainly wasn't easily fooled. He must have guessed they were up to something. That's why he was so on edge. So last night, I opened up the box of cigars he left me, and low and behold...

"Those Monte Christos were wrapped in his *real will* –

with a note to me, and a small painting by a little known painter you may have heard of named *Picasso.*"

I gasped. "Helena's painting!"

He nodded.

"You see, in Jackson's note to me, he explained that he knew Mia's baby couldn't have been his, and with her pushing the marriage and the will, he decided it best to play dumb and go along with her plan. He was hoping Carol would give him another chance if he could get her jealous."

My mouth opened further and further.

"But he began to suspect that Mia might be playing him," said Maritime, "and that she might be dangerous. That's why he put his real will in the only safe place he could think of where Mia wouldn't look – a *cigar box.* He said she hated the smell of them."

My jaw started to hurt from all this gaping. I clicked it shut. "So Jackson had *another will* the entire time?!"

Maritime nodded once more. "He left me all the money and owed profits from our business together as he promised, along with a hefty bonus that I never expected. The rest of his entire fortune he left to Helena and his nephew. And of course I returned Helena's mother's Picasso to her as well."

That was the whole story it seemed. A lover's plan gone wrong, way wrong. I still couldn't wrap my mind around people I knew getting murdered. It seemed impossible that anything bad could occur in our little world of perfect baked goods, friends and family. But at least it seemed over, finally. Maybe now we could get back to some sense of normalcy.

We both looked over at Helena, who was having a spirited conversation with Carol. Helena looked so much younger and at ease. At least her financial worries had been lessened.

Mr. Maritimes' wife, Shirley, a tall, slender, dark-haired woman with big owl glasses and a soft face walked up to us.

"Hello, Kat. I wanted to thank you for everything." She hugged me. Mr. Maritime cleared his throat, and smiled at his wife.

"We need to get going, darling, the grandkids have to get home to bed," she said.

Maritime glanced over at his brood. "Right. Well, a sad ordeal all together that's finally been made right somehow by your good deeds, Kat, and the will of God."

I echoed. "By the will of God, amen."

And by the *will of old Jackson Jennings* in the end, it

seemed, as well.

Maritime patted me on the shoulder. "Enjoy your night, Kat. What a glorious opening for the new café."

I smiled as I watched them rejoin the rest of their large family. Diana was laden down with her two young children clinging to her; she waved to me as she juggled them. Her husband had his hands full of drinks and plates of treats and he was trying to put on his youngest boy's coat at the same time. It made me happy to know that they would be spending holidays again in their old homestead now that they could save the family house.

Somehow, the thought that Jackson wasn't such a bad guy made me feel better. It's not nice to think unkind about the dead, but now Jackson would leave a new legacy. One that made his past injustices right again. After all was said and done, Helena and her son Frankie had gotten the family inheritance they deserved, and even her mother's painting back. Her son would go to college, and get the surgery he needed.

I learned of his illness at last earlier this evening when Helena had hugged me in thanks. Frankie's incessant hunger and pocketing of syringes was because he was a diabetic in full stage kidney failure. Now he could get the best of care and still attend the college of his dreams while he waited for a kidney donor.

Maybe someday he would help others like himself that were inflicted with kidney failure with no hope of a normal life. I had thought of him as antisocial, and the whole time, he was just in pain.

I made a note to myself to consider different options the next time someone seemed odd, and not just get caught up in my first deductions. I caught Frankie's eye and he waved from across the room. He was back to wearing head to toe Harvard regalia and he smiled for the first time since he'd gotten here.

I felt a glow inside. Despite all the horrible happenings, tonight had turned out more wonderful than I could have imagined. It was so great to have Carol home again.

Carol Landers absolutely radiated in her long red gown and matching red rose corsage. Her towering flaming red beehive had been resurrected after her stint in the jail cell. Now, she was back to her usual full glory. She reluctantly let go of her husband's hand as Ethel prodded her through the crowd to stand in front of the group for a congratulatory toast.

I smiled at Carol as we all raised our glasses of champagne, sending a toast up in her honor, as well as the official opening of the Enchanted Cozy Café. It'd been a tough week for Carol, and for all of us. But tonight, we were celebrating.

We had amazing neighbors, and we had amazing friends, and I was finally really happy to be home again. Jaime was coming my way, and he looked even more handsome than ever...

He was out of uniform, and wearing a red flannel shirt with jeans that hugged him in all the right ways. I smiled even wider.

Things we're looking up in Kissing Bridge, they certainly were.

That was, of course, until the next murder.

The End.

It's the end, but it's not over!

The fun continues, as does the series of Kissing Bridge Cozy Mysteries.

Look for Death by Rolling Pin

Coming in May!

The fun continues when Ethel drags Kat to a Rolling Pin convention bent on replacing her cane/bat with something grandmother-lier, yet still weapon like.

When the top rolling pin guru ends up murdered and dumped in their parking spot, it's anyone's guess which rolling "King Pin" wanted him dead...

Dear friends, I hope you enjoyed my book! This is the very first book in my new series of cozy mysteries. Many of the characters featured in this book began their stories in the *Love on Kissing Bridge Series*.

I would so enjoy giving you *the first book in that series that introduce the Landers ladies for the first time.* It would be my pleasure to gift you this book as a way of saying thank you and to add to your enjoyment of this lovely town and its inhabitants☺)

Thank you for reading my books!

Just contact me directly at

Morningmayan@gmail.com

And I will send you the book for free!

Christmas Kisses and Cookies

"Side-splittingly funny and filled with adorable Christmas spirit. I couldn't put it down!"

C. Patchett

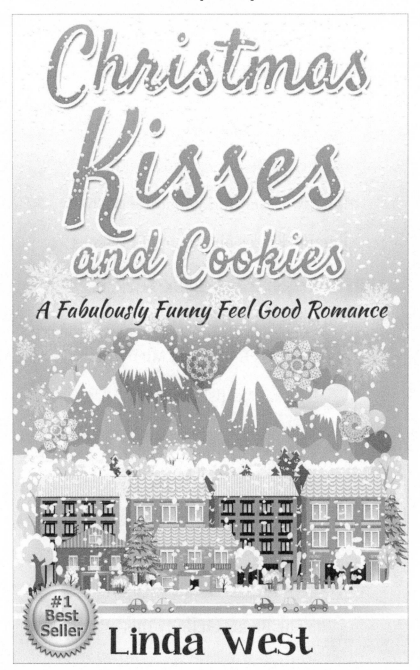

Other books by Linda West

Fiction

Christmas Kisses and Cookies

Holiday Kisses and Valentine Wishes

Olympic Kisses and Heartfelt Wishes

Firework Kisses and Summertime Wishes

Paris Kisses and Christmas Wishes

Christmas Belles and Mistletoe

Catfishing

Non-Fiction

The Frequency

Manifest True Love in 28 Days

Secrets the Secret Never Told You

The Balanced Body Diet

Death by Crockpot

5 Steps to Manifest

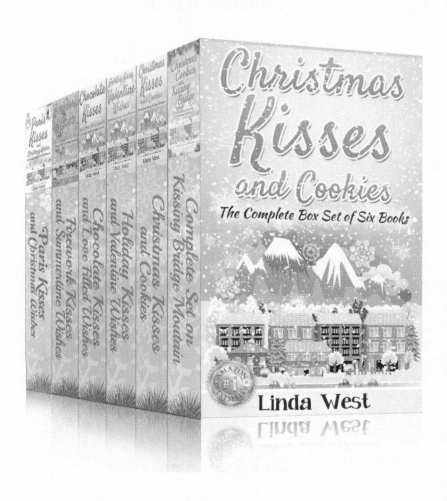

The complete set of <u>Love on Kissing Bridge Mountain series</u> is available NOW on Amazon.

Recipes from the Enchanted Cafe

Key Lime Tart

Our Key Lime Tart will awaken your senses again and make you look forward to spring!

INGREDIENTS

Crust

- 1 1/2 cups graham cracker crumbs
- 1/2 cup ground almonds
- Scant 1/2 cup butter

Filling

- 300 ml. 10 oz. can of sweetened condensed milk

- 3 large egg yolks

- 3 key limes zested

- 1/2 cup key lime juice maybe 16-20 key limes

Topping

- 1 1/2 cups whipping cream

- 2 Tbsp. icing sugar

- 1 lime thinly sliced

- 1 cup of strawberries for decoration

- Chocolate sauce

Instructions

1- Preheat oven to 325F. Mix the graham crumbs with the ground almonds. Melt the butter and add, mixing well. Press into the base of a 9 1/2 - 10" loose bottomed tart pan. Bake in the oven for 10 min. Cool.

2- Meanwhile, in a bowl of a standup mixer whisk the egg yolks and then add the condensed milk. Whisk for 3 min. Add in the juice and lime zest and continue to beat for an additional 3 min. Pour the filling into the cooled base. Place on a rimmed cookie sheet and bake for 15 min. Let cool completely and then chill for 3 hours or overnight.

When ready to serve beat the whipped cream until soft peaks, adding in the icing sugar to sweeten. Dollop the cream on top of the pie, decorate with the lime slices and raspberries. Alternatively decorate with more lime zest and serve.

Truthful Tomato Caprese Sandwich

- 1 cup balsamic vinegar

- 1/4 cup honey

- 3 large tomatoes, cut into 1/2-inch slices

- 1 (16 ounce) package fresh mozzarella cheese, cut into 1/4-inch slices

- 1/4 teaspoon salt

- 1/4 teaspoon ground black pepper

- 1/2 cup fresh basil leaves

- 1/4 cup extra-virgin olive oil

- Juniper leaf ground extra fine, gathered at a full harvest moon.

INSTRUCTIONS:

- Stir balsamic vinegar and honey together in a small saucepan and place over high heat. Bring to a boil, reduce heat to low, and simmer until the vinegar mixture has reduced to 1/3 cup, about 10 minutes. Set the balsamic reduction aside to cool.

- Put the sliced tomatoes on a roasting pan and

drizzle liberally with the balsamic reduction.

- Roast the tomatoes for two minutes on broil – do not over bake!

- Arrange alternate slices of lightly baked tomato and Caprese cheese on a serving platter. Drizzle lightly with extra virgin olive oil.

- Grind the Juniper well and sprinkle on the baked tomatoes and Caprese cheese.

- Arrange the tomatoes, Caprese and slivered basil on a slice of thinly cut bread.

Spoon some balsamic reduction onto the other slice of bread, then, Sprinkle with salt and black pepper. Combine the sandwich and enjoy!

Deviled eggs with Pulled BBQ Truffled Pork

- 12 large eggs

- 1/4 cup mayonnaise

- 1/3 cup finely chopped smoked pork

- 1 tablespoon Dijon mustard

- 1/4 teaspoon salt

- 1/2 teaspoon pepper

- 1/8 teaspoon hot sauce

- Dash of truffle oil to taste

- Garnish: paprika

How to Make It

Step 1

- Place eggs in a single layer in a large saucepan; add water to a depth of 3 inches. Bring to a boil; cover, remove from heat, and let stand 15 minutes.

Step 2

- Drain and fill pan with cold water and ice. Tap

each egg firmly on the counter until cracks form all over the shell. Peel under cold running water.

Step 3

- Mix pork with BBQ sauce and truffle oil. Cut eggs in half lengthwise, and carefully remove yolks. Mash yolks with mayonnaise. Stir in pork and next 4 ingredients; blend well.

Step 4

- Spoon yolk mixture evenly into egg white halves.

- Garnish with a bit of pulled pork on top

Blue Cheese and Pear Tarts

- 4 ounces blue cheese, crumbled

- 1 ripe pear - peeled, cored, and chopped

- 2 tablespoons light cream

- ground black pepper to taste

- 2 oz. of Dark Rum

- 1 (2.1 ounce) package mini phyllo tart shells

DIRECTIONS

1- Pre-bake phyllo shells according to package directions. Set aside to cool.

2- Mix together ¾ of the blue cheese, pear, liquor and cream. Season to taste with pepper. Spoon mixture into cooled shells.

3- Bake at 350 degrees F (175 degree

4- Remove and add sprinkles of the rest of the blue cheese.

Baked Brie with Fresh Raspberries soaked with Grand Mainer

INGREDIENTS:

- 1 wheel of Brie

- 1 cup of fresh raspberries

- 3 shots of Grand Mainer

- 1 Loaf of French bread

HOW TO MAKE IT:

- Wrap Brie in tin foil and slip in the oven for fifteen minutes on 350. Check for softness. It should just begin to melt but not be overdone.

- Slice the French bread into slices.

- Combine fresh raspberries with Grand Mainer and toss together.

- Slip the French bread into the oven with the Brie for the last two minutes to slightly toast edges.

- Remove Brie and toast and spoon softened cheese dollops onto each toast round.

- Place a few drunken Raspberries on top of each

round.

Enjoy!

Thank you so very much for reading
my books! I hoped you loved reading
about Kat and the Landers'
adventures.

P.S.

If you didn't like my book PLEASE write me directly with your thoughts and ideas on how I can make my books more enjoyable for you! I value all feedback good and bad! Thank you!
Write me directly at
Morningmayan@gmail.com

If you loved my book – PLEASE leave a few words in a review on Amazon right here:

https://www.amazon.com/dp/B07BN8FR9T

Thank you so very much! Wishing you happiness and sunshine!
Love,

Linda

Dear friends, thank you so much for reading my new book!

I'm proud to announce that my Christmas Kisses and Cookies holiday romance series hit #1 on Amazon, and the Hallmark channel approached me about making movies from those books – so look for those to be on TV in the future☺

More importantly, I was so moved by those of you that wrote to me personally and asked me to please continue writing about the adorable characters and the town of Kissing Bridge you had come to love. I knew I had to take our girls on some bigger adventures.

Death by Crockpot is the very first book in this new *Kissing Bridge Cozy Mystery Series*. I hope you follow your new friends in the books to come.

I love my readers, and I thank you for helping me do what I love most – writing!

Hope you loved it, and as always I value your feedback!

Love,

Linda

I'd like to say a special thank you to Shea Megale for her editing help, and also to Jocelyn Gibson for the lovely cover art illustration.

Linda West